INKED IN
ILLUSIONS

INKED IN ILLUSIONS

SHORT STORIES

DEVASHISH ACHARYA

PARTRIDGE
A Penguin Random House Company

To order additional copies of this book, contact
Partridge India
000 800 10062 62
orders.india@partridgepublishing.com

www.partridgepublishing.com/india

Contents

For Aahan

Sing in me, Muse, and through me tell the stories…

Acknowledgement

First and foremost, I would like to thank Maa, Baba, Di and Aparesh Da for their continued support and encouragement. I feel proud when I say that my parents shared my dream and never gave up on me. Dad, thank you for inculcating the habit of reading and writing in me; in fact, most of my creations are inspired by your own works. Maa, thanks for keeping me motivated and most importantly for never comparing me with the other kids, who were apparently studying hard to become astronauts, while I kept scribbling stars in my notebook. Di, thank you for being such a patient reader even when you rarely understood what I wrote. Aparesh Da, thanks for withstanding my whining and cribbing all this while when I was trying to decide on my career path.

Now, I would like to thank my friend and editor, Devika Khare. Had she not gone through my works with a fine-tooth comb, my book definitely would have taken the form of a reference book titled "The silliest mistakes in English". In this regard, I would also like to thank Aditi Bhattacharjee for proofreading my stories and ensuring that they were safe enough to be read.

I would like to extend my heartfelt gratitude to Dheeraja, Avisha, Ashish, Ravi, Shefali, Dushyant, Darshit, Lakshay, Bhawna, Nitika, Sangeeta, Loni and Mona just because they wanted their names in the book. On a serious note, I thank them for being consistently patient readers and I thank them for providing their feedback on each story that has led to this final book.

Given my weak memory, I might have missed a few names, but I take this opportunity to thank all my friends, family and relatives for their love, support and motivation. This book is our effort, not just mine.

PREFACE

Have you ever seen a flock of flying birds and wondered if they knew their destination? Do they always know which way they are heading? Can they see beyond the mist of uncertainties that obscures their route? Or do they simply let their whims guide their wings? Don't they ever get lost? But then, is getting lost such a bad thing? After all, we sometimes discover better and more wonderful places when we allow ourselves to get lost.

Thus, I too allowed my thoughts to wander astray. And I realized that the beauty of our lives lies in the unpredictability that we face at every turn. Sometimes like a generous old woman, sometimes like a cruel stranger, sometimes like a smiling friend and sometimes like an ugly portrait, life takes countless different forms to amaze us all.

A new story begins every second, and every moment can be a new plot twist. This exactly is the theme of this book.

And the thirteen short stories in this book, each belonging to a different genre, are my way of paying regards to the uncertainties of life.

Now, I am releasing a flock of birds and all of them are ready to fly towards unknown destinations. Are you ready to take flight with them? If yes, *Bon Voyage...*

Moon-Mad

A fleck of moon brimmed up his cup
and tides of thoughts rose high,
the nocturnal nymphs of nostalgia
flickered with the dancing lights.
A glint of dream came floating in
and the woods howled inside,
figments romanced the firmament
as stars turned into fireflies.
The chaotic crescendo of crickets
echoed the stories of night,
the starry infinity beyond the stars
found place in two sleepless eyes.

The lunar lunacy of life filled in
his perversely embellished room,
the moon-mad, through the mirror cracks,
smiled at the broken piece of moon.

WISH MAKERS

Dim lit was her room as if it was trying to get in sync with her feelings. Tanu was sitting on her bed; her head was dug in her knees. Her phone buzzed to break the eternal silence. She knew that it was her mom. It was the ninth time since the evening that she was calling Tanu, no call being answered. Tanu finally lifted up her head, reached her phone and switched it off. Through bloodshot eyes, she looked at the watch; 1:37 AM it was. She stood up, wiped the drops of sorrow off her face and threw a glance at the letters and cards lying on the floor. An hour ago, she had fed most of the cards and letters to fire. These remaining ones needed to be reduced to ashes as well, but she was too tired for that. She needed her remaining energy for something else. She had got more important issues to take care of.

With a loud sigh, she went up to her desk and started writing..

Mom/Dad,

I know that it's too late to say anything, and I know that I should have listened to you when you said that you didn't trust that guy whom I have been calling the love of my life. But none of that matters now. I feel betrayed. So much have I been drinking from the bottle of life that I didn't even realize when I completely lost my senses. Now, when I look back, I feel horrible seeing myself getting wasted again and again and again. Now, perhaps, I will never be able to sober up. I misused all the freedom that you gave to me. I am sorry. I feel drowsy, and I want to sleep now. If you are reading this, then it means that the sleeping pills have already put me to rest.

I know that the world will call me a coward after my suicide, and I wish that there was any other way. I wish that I died in an accident or some disease took me. I just wish to die before committing suicide.

Tanu

PS: No one is responsible for my suicide.

"*I wish I had just died… I don't want to commit suicide… I wish… I wish…*" Tanu could hold back her tears and screams no more. Next day, she knew, was the day when she would relieve herself from the mortal sufferings. After all, the next day was Monday; neighbors would be gone for work and her cook would come late in the evening. By the time anyone realized, it would all be over.

Next Morning:

It was 9:00 AM when she left her house. There was a druggist, she knew, who gave medicines without ever bothering to check for a doctor's prescription, and lucky enough for her, insomnia had become the new plague. Almost every fourth corporate employee suffered from it. No one would doubt her if she asked for sleeping pills from the druggist.

As she entered the chemist store, she saw a man coughing and yelling over his phone, *"What do you mean by you got late? We never delay our deliveries. Okay, let me see what I can do, but Boss won't be very happy."* Even though he was well dressed, from his face, it was evident that he was suffering from inside- a tall, lanky fellow with a clean shaven, wrinkled face and shallow, deep, discerning eyes. She wondered how people prioritized things in life.

As she had thought, never did the druggist ask for any prescription. *"That went well,"* she thought as she came out of the store. Inside her head, she started rehearsing her own 'farewell', but her thoughts were interrupted when she saw a man leaning over the road while a truck directly headed towards him. It was the same man she saw at the chemist store. She ran towards him to pull him away just in the nick of time, thus saving him from an accident. As she got him back on his feet, she yelled at him,

"Are you mad, sir? Or do you want to die?"

"No and no," the man replied as he innocently smiled, *"On the contrary, I want to live."*

Tanu, confused, was about to walk away, remembering that she had her own priorities right now. But she stopped as she heard the man speak.

"*Neuroblastoma, they say, I am suffering from. The heat… it just got my nerve.*"

"*Then why don't you go to your home and take rest? Or go sit with a doctor? Why do you think you are working in this heat?*" Tanu bluntly jeered.

"*If I stop working, then who will feed my schizophrenic mother and who will pay for my medicines? If not for me, then at least for my mother, I have to work till I am alive. I cannot run away from my responsibilities. That would be selfish,*" replied the man, still struggling to catch his breath. "*Thank you, ma'am; thanks for saving me today.*"

"*Don't you have anyone else to look after you and your mother?*" Tanu somehow felt everything directed at her.

"*Have? No. Had? Yes. But then she abandoned me the day doctors told me that I was suffering from cancer.*" His expressions hardened but he still managed a smile.

The statement, somehow, left Tanu dumbfounded for a while as she struggled to find a response to what she had just heard.

"*I… I am sorry. I shouldn't have yelled at you. I really didn't know what you were going through,*" she fumbled as she spoke.

"*It's alright. I have learned living this way.*"

"*Not everyone is as courageous as you are, sir.*" Tanu smiled for the first time in the last countless hours. Her reason for pain had been put to shame by this man.

"*It's not about being tough. You know what, life is the greatest addiction. It's just that some people don't know how to make the best out of this addiction. We all drink from the bottle of life…"*

"*Sorry, what?*" Tanu interrupted, startled at this bizarre choice of words.

"*What?*"

"*Oh, nothing… just a coincidence… Please continue.*"

"*Yeah,*" continued the man, "*we sometimes lose our senses while drinking from that bottle and do some terrible things; things that haunt us all through our lives. Sometimes, we feel sick and sometimes, it seems that our world has turned upside down, but again, sobering up is in our hands. And it is important to sober up so that we can lose our senses all over again. That is the beauty of life.*" He paused and looked at her. "*Sorry, that was too much philosophy. I think I have bored you already! My work, you see, teaches me a lot of philosophy.*" He was interrupted by a phone-call, which he apologetically received.

"*Yes sir,*" he spoke, "*the package is ready for delivery? Perfect. We will receive it right away, without further delay.*" He disconnected and apologized with a sheepish smile.

'*Who can even imagine about his sufferings behind the mask of his zeal?*' Tanu thought to herself and smiled with guilt.

"*Work, you see… It's time for you to go, ma'am. I will take your leave. Here's our company card if anyone ever needs. And once again… thanks,*" the man said to her as he handed her a card. Tanu looked calm now.

The man said goodbye and started walking away from her. Tanu silently took out a paper from her pocket; it was her suicide note. She looked at it with utter repugnance and threw it away across the road. Then, she started crossing the road, unaware that the man had stopped walking and was watching her now, frequently throwing glances at his wrist watch with a very different smile on his face. But Tanu's eyes were now on the card this man gave to her. She was baffled by what was written on it. She stopped in the middle of the road and turned back to see the man looking at his watch. He looked up at her and smiled. Then, he looked at the distant car speeding towards Tanu. The last thing Tanu saw, before the car hit her, was a man with a wicked smile waving her goodbye.

As the crowd gathered to beat the driver of the car, the man walked up to see Tanu's lifeless body, and then, from the road, he picked up a piece of paper that had got Tanu's blood all over it. He gently folded it and kept it in his pocket- Tanu's suicide note. He, then, started walking away as he made a phone-call and spoke, "*Boss… job done. We delivered her wish to her. Yeah! She was surprised.*" He laughed. "*The guy also got his wish. He wanted to get rid of his girlfriend. It's just that he didn't know that he himself was going to kill her in a road accident,*" he spoke with a proud smile, "*Wait a second.*" He paused as he overheard a couple fighting on the other side of the road.

A woman was cursing her husband, "*I wish you rot in hell.*"

"*Hey boss, you heard that? I think we got another client,*" he spoke and laughed as he disappeared in the crowd.

On the accident spot, the cops found three interesting things- the first two being a bottle of sleeping pills (no medical prescription was found) and a bill showing where she got the pills from. Few cops had already been sent for the druggist. But the third thing, which they could make nothing of, was a business card. On one side of the card was written- 'Wish Makers' and on the other side, some simple, sophisticated words:

Make a Wish
We Are *Always* Listening

ACATALEPSY

*"She had more truth in her nicotine-soaked eyes
than the screaming carcasses of the millions alive"*

She took out a small mirror from her bag and checked her face under the flickering streetlight, which seemed to be in no mood to lighten up this night. The cold, winter-night wind brushed against her face and the scars beneath her extravagant makeup brutally screamed back to life. Convinced that the brushes and colors were successful in concealing the torments beneath, she put the mirror back and checked her bag one last time to make sure that she hadn't missed anything. Among other items, there were mostly medicines, especially painkillers.

Nancy; that was what they called her, and like every other night, this night also, someone was waiting for her.

But this night was a bit different. Other nights, she would know who she was going to meet and how that person would treat her. But she was not so sure about her tonight's client.

"*Delusional!*" one of her co-workers had told her.

"*He was such a gentleman!*" another had remarked.

"*Bloody maniac; I had to be admitted in emergency after what he did to me,*" one more had informed.

So now, she was not so sure about her client's mood and how she would be treated. It was not that she was new to sadism. In fact, seven years in this line had shown her horrors enough for a lifetime. But a human she was; and like every human, she too felt pain and was afraid of it.

She took out a card that read the address of an old manor at the end of the street- the kind of house some bureaucrats and politicians kept with the intention of storing black money and performing other evil rituals of life. She just kept dragging her feet with unsure steps and a hope, '*Tonight would be different.*'

Five times, she rang the doorbell, but came no reply. Before she could ring the bell again, came a voice from inside,

"*Who is there?*"

"*Sir, I am from Asterix Services,*" she replied.

"*So?*" inquired the voice.

"*You gave us a call, sir. You were in need of our services. You… called us is this morning,*" she replied, sounding confused.

"*I do not require your services, whatever they may be,*" bluntly said the voice.

"*But sir, you know that it does not…*" The door opened before she could complete. Out came a young man with a face so innocent that she felt like telling him to go back and shut the door so that he could be safe from the wild world outside. But then she remembered a simple reality - her life had never ceased to surprise her.

"May I come inside?" she asked.

"Have you come alone?" the man asked as he peeped outside.

'Delusional,' she thought, but said, *"No, I took a cab."*

"Come inside," he guided her inside and shut the door.

"So… Are you Mr. Shetty?" she asked as she walked in.

"Funny!" he laughed and scoffed, *"You don't even know the most popular politician of the town… Yes… I am Shetty."* He pulled a chair near the fireplace as he boasted.

'Politicians never make any law to protect me, nor can I exercise any right like other people do. Why should I even give a damn who you are?' she thought, but said instead, *"No sir… I have come here for the first time."*

The man looked at his watch, smiled, motioned her to sit on the chair near the fireplace and said, *"Yeah, that I can see."*

'So, he is a gentleman,' she thought, pleased at how he asked her to sit.

"So…" he started as he looked at her with thoughtful eyes, *"What do they call you?"*

"Nancy," came a well-rehearsed reply.

"Nancy? Is that what your parents named you, if you ever had them, of course?"

A long time it had been since anyone had called her by her real name. It took her a minute or two to remember her own name.

"Koel… That is what my parents named me."

"That's a beautiful name." He paused, went up to her and lifted up her face. *"Now, I would like you to answer a few questions, and I would like you to be completely honest with me, or else… believe me, dear girl… you are going to regret."* Such was the tone of his voice and such was the glare in his eyes that they naturally provoked hatred and fear at the same time. Nancy sensed a chill down her spine.

'Sadists,' she thought, *'are always turned on by the stories of sufferings. And a sadist this guy is… definitely…'* but asked, *"What do you want to know?"*

"To start with… why, when and how did you end up in this… this profession?"

As the memories started haunting her again, she started putting them into words, *"I was eleven when I lost my mother and my father was in the military. He would often stay out of home because of service, so he married another woman to fill in for my mother. But this woman, apparently my 'new mother', she would torture me in his absence. But that was not enough. Life gave me another surprise. It was during a military operation that we received the news of my father's demise."* Her eyes welled up, but she continued, *"That was the time when my stepmother's brother came and started staying with us… a filthy, bloody drunkard, he was. He would abuse and beat me and…"* She choked on her own tears.

"Continue," the man calmly said, *"Don't stop now."*

She looked up at him with utter disgust in her teary eyes and started again, *"By the age of sixteen, I was twice raped by him as if her sister's torments were not enough. Then… Then I tried to run away… I was caught, tortured and handed over to a pimp in exchange for money. By the age of eighteen, I was already getting destroyed by my clients… It's been seven years since…"* She could speak no more.

"You said you tried to run away from your home. Ever tried to run away from this brothel of yours?" the man asked, biting his lips.

"What?" She was unsure if she should answer.

"I asked if you ever tried to run away in the past seven years." There was an unsettling calmness in his voice- something that would sound soothingly creepy to a person in distress.

"I did," she replied, scared of course, *"But I was caught, tortured, beaten, bound and thrown in a junkyard, naked, where I almost died of pain, cold, thirst and hunger while some worms had already started feeding on me."*

"So why didn't you try to run away again?" he asked, still calm.

"Because Mister… I think you missed a simple point. I don't have money and thus, nowhere to go. And if I try to run away again, I will be caught and tortured again, and I am sure I don't want that to happen… again." Her voice failed to conceal her anger.

"Okay… okay…" The man seemed to be amused as he chuckled and smiled. *"So what do we do now?"* He again lifted up her face.

"What do you want me to do?" Nancy asked in a firm, unfaltering tone.

"First," he looked at his watch as he spoke, *"I would like you to wash that makeup off your face."*

"Sorry?"

"You heard me. In any case your tears have revealed the scars beneath your makeup." He stood up and showed her the way to washroom.

A few minutes later, she was in the washroom, terrified to see even her own reflection in the mirror… her brutalized face. She had, by now, lost track of what was going on. She once again checked her bag to see if all the necessary items were there. *"Tonight would be different,"* she reassured the person in the mirror.

As she walked back into the room, she saw the man talking over phone. Seeing her, he disconnected the call and walked up to her. With slow, shaky steps, he went closer to her.

"They did this to you? Your clients?" His hands were all over her scars now, and Nancy sensed a distantly familiar pain in his voice.

"Don't let anyone hurt you again," he spoke, softly.

"What?" Startled, she was.

"Do you have a habit of reconfirming what I say to you?" He smiled. *"You heard me,"* he said as he walked up to the table and opened a small bag, *"Here is some money, enough for you to leave this place and start afresh."*

"I… but… you…" Nancy kept on fumbling.

"It's okay… You don't have to say anything. You deserve a better life. Just go. Go before I change my mind." His voice was calm, soft and kind.

Before she knew it, she was crying like an eleven year old that she once was, and on her knees, she fell. He lifted her up and wiped off her tears. For her, there was nothing around but a void… just silence… and when this silence got over, he guided her out of the door, handed her the bag and said *"Leave Nancy behind… Goodbye, Koel."* Koel tried to smile but her tears won the race. She started walking away as the man closed the door.

She opened her own bag and took out a knife. *'Enough,'* she had thought earlier this evening, *'I will end my sufferings; I won't let anyone hurt me again; I will take away my life. But before I do that, I will definitely take down one of those sadists.'* But then again, it seemed she was right; her life never ceased to surprise her.

Cold wind still blew, but it didn't hurt her scars anymore because now, she only felt the warmth of tears on her wounds-both inside and out; tears that eventually lightened up her face with a smile. As she walked past a series of flickering streetlights, she sensed a new dawn upon her.

Back at the manor, an hour later, the man stood up as he read a text on his phone screen:

"Highway Security Down. Move."

He smiled as he pulled over a coat and went inside a room where two men in uniform were lying down, bound and gagged- apparently the security guards of the manor. He smiled, looking down at them and lifted up two bags. Then he walked out of the house. Moments later, he was walking towards a car parked across the road. As he got into the car, he heard a muffled voice from the back seat. He looked back to see a bald, old man bound and gagged. His head was bleeding profusely.

"Hello, Mr. Shetty. It seems that you are finally awake," he scornfully said as he put his hands on the steering wheel. *"You would probably be glad to know that your black money saved a soul tonight."* He started the engine of the car. *"As for the rest of your money,"* he threw a glance at the two bags which he brought from the manor and continued, *"they are going to feed some needy. And as for you,"* he turned back to look at Mr. Shetty's face and whispered, *"I am going to beat you, torture you a little, strip you naked and then, I will throw you in some junkyard for rodents to feed on you."* He winked and grinned as he saw terror in Shetty's eyes. Then he started driving off as a loud music inside the car killed Shetty's muffled screams.

The Ghosts

The night was dark and stormy, and the clouds roared and poured. Ajeet Roy was sitting with his college friend, Shubham Dhar, in a poorly furnished living room. As the sky blazed again, the lights went off.

"Pernicious!" exclaimed Dhar as he lit up a cigarette, *"Load-shedding was the only thing missing from this devil of a stormy night. Care for a cigarette, Roy?"* He offered a cigarette to Roy.

"No, thanks. I have quit and so should you." Roy forced a smile.

"Really? You have changed quite a lot. I mean you look old, and you have quit all the good habits. Is everything alright with you?" Dhar mockingly asked as he threw away the burning match in agony as it almost burnt his fingers.

"Yes, yes of course."

"Come on, old man! Don't look and sound so malaise. It has been an aeon since I last saw you in college. Where the hell have you been all this while?"

"I was experimenting with the lives of my students," Roy replied with a smile.

"Professor," Dhar coughed and spoke, *"Who could even think that you, a retard, could ever become a professor?"*

"Moumita," Dhar shouted, *"bring some candles. I don't want to spend the entire evening in the dark. I am already spending my life in it."*

"Moumita?" enquired Roy.

"Yes, the maid who opened the door for you."

"Oh! I see," Roy remarked as he cleared his throat, *"And what do you mean by you are spending your life in darkness?"*

Dhar's face went grave. Then he asked, *"Do you know what I do for a living, professor?"*

"I thought you were a writer?"

"Yes, that I am, but I am not." Dhar promptly replied.

"What does that…" Before Roy could complete, a woman walked into the room with lit candles in her hands. As she placed the candles on the table, Roy saw her face and observed that her face perfectly complemented the gloominess of the room. She threw a glance at Roy, quickly turned away her face and walked out of the room.

"I am a writer," Dhar grunted, *"but a ghost writer. In fact, even the term 'ghost-writer' won't be aptly applicable to my situation."*

"What?" Roy questioned, curiously leaning towards Dhar.

"I use to write for other writers. I use to write the stories but they use to brand my stories with their names. They get them

published; they sell them; they earn all the fame, and I only earn some scanty commission."

"*And why would you let that happen?*" Roy asked with surprise gripping his face. He waited for Dhar's reply, but none came. So he asked again, "*I want to know what happened to you, Dhar. What is your story?*"

"*I had just completed my graduation,*" started Dhar, "*and I was ambitious. You know how I was, Roy, don't you? I never had many friends to speak to. I just had my little world of imagination where nothing was mean and bad, and I never even bothered when people called me a freak.*" He let out a sigh and continued, "*Sometimes, you know, I even doubted if people around me were aware of my existence. It was as if I was nothing but a ghost to all of them. Only those who knew me well were aware of my presence. But I knew that I had one thing that others failed to possess- 'my words', and I was sure that one day this world would know me because of my stories.*" After a long pause, he again started, "*But I was wrong. I never knew that the world beyond my imagination was so different, so cruel. I tried to approach many publishers, but all in vain. I knew that I could not do well in any other job. I, to be honest, knew nothing else but writing, so I kept on hunting. I kept on hunting till I had almost given up on my faith. Then, one day, a publisher agreed to meet me. He, in fact, praised all my works and gave me another big shot's address. He said that this guy could change my life.*" Dhar stopped and stared at the flickering candlelight.

"*What happened then?*" Roy asked.

"*The guy changed my life,*" Dhar forced a pained smile as he mumbled, "*This guy, I remember, was a big name amongst writers, and he too seemed to like my works. He liked them so much that he promised me that he would make me rich. He gave me a small sum of money as an advance before the stories were edited and published. I gave him all of my stories; I gave him all my original manuscripts; a fool I was."* He paused, looked up at Roy and said, *"You know what? I, for a moment, felt like l was living in another of my imaginary worlds; everything was just so perfect for me at that moment. But the happiness didn't last long. Months passed and I did not receive any call from this guy, so I went to meet him. And... and he humiliated me, saying that my works were rubbish and that he had been very kind to not notice it earlier. He even said that the publishers had thrown away my works in the trash. And then, he shut his door on my face. All my works, my lifetime of creations, everything was gone. I was naïve and fool to hand him my original manuscripts. I could not even bear the thought of them lying at the bottom of a trash pile."* He stopped before his voice rose again, *"It was a summer evening, and I was travelling by train. I was returning back to my small town where there was an opening for a clerical position in a local company. A co-passenger was reading a book. I noticed that it was by the same author who humiliated me. I borrowed the book from him and started reading, and it was then that it struck me. That bastard was selling my work and earning fame- each page, each sentence, each word, all my creations, exactly the same as I wrote them. Then I saw the back-cover of the book. It appeared he had won several awards for this book."* He paused and then continued, *"I took a train back to the city from the next station and immediately, I went up to him, but he was not surprised. He welcomed me. He first offered me food and wine. And then, he made another offer."*

"What offer?" Roy asked, getting restless.

"*He wanted to employ me as his ghost writer and he promised me good compensations- sheer audacity! I, obviously, turned down the offer and straight went to find a lawyer. But who would believe me? I didn't have the original copies with me and thus, it was a weak case for all the lawyers. No one would take me. I fought, I broke, I lost and with time, I realized that in the jungle out there, all the fierce animals hunted together; no publisher would take me.*"

"*Then?*" Roy inquired.

Dhar clenched his teeth and replied, "*Then I started selling my ideas to writers other than this guy. This pissed him off badly, and I really enjoyed it. It was as if this was my way of revenge- creating players who could put this guy out of the market. And it did happen. But I didn't even realize that I was only hopping on a bed of quicksand by doing such a thing. Soon, I became what I am today- a ghost writer, a person who doesn't exist at all. I became what I used to think of myself during college.*"

"*So, you never tried to approach publishers again?*" Roy asked as he poured water into the two glasses kept on the table.

"*As I said, I am a ghost. I do not exist. Let's talk about something else. We have really met after such a long time. You remember all that fun we three used to have together, you, me and Riya?*"

"*Hey! Where is Riya? You married her, right? I could not even attend your wedding.*" Roy took out a bottle of pills from his pocket, carefully keeping it out of Dhar's sight.

Dhar's face went grave and white. His expressions tensed as if he was trying to remember something.

"I did marry Riya, but me… my wife left me when my life was at the peak of crisis… Riya, her name was…" Dhar struggled with words. He seemed to be confused, under some sort of stress.

"Was your wife beautiful Dhar?" Roy asked as he again threw a glance at his watch.

"She…" He started as dizziness started taking over him, *"Wait. I remember… No… Right… She was… Oh! God… She is…"* Dhar tried to speak so many things but couldn't. He started breathing heavily, holding his head. His head was throbbing. He was not able to see anything. He tried to scream in agony, but couldn't.

Roy quickly got up, took out a pill from the bottle and shoved it down Dhar's throat. Within moments, Dhar was sleeping like a baby. After a series of other drugs and injections, Roy started looking at the papers on the table. Then, he started searching drawers and cupboard. Then he made his way downstairs towards the kitchen. The maid was sitting there, he knew.

"Riya," he called.

The maid looked up at him and asked, *"Is he already asleep?"*

"Yes," replied Roy.

"Any progress, Roy?" the woman with grief-stricken eyes, the maid, Riya, asked.

"Better than last week, I believe." Roy handed the bottle of pills to Riya. *"In fact, today, he almost remembered your name and face. I think that he even realized that it is you, his wife, not some maid. But he broke down before he could speak more. Every time he tries to remember you or your face, he just gets stressed out."*

"And he won't remember this all when he wakes up tomorrow." There were tears in Riya's eyes.

"I don't know. It has been a few months since it began, right? And on many occasions, he remembers a few things, but then you know... he does not remember anything when he wakes up. One thing that he never remembers is his accident... as if it never happened." He paused, looked at Riya with doubtful eyes and asked, *"I want to ask something personal, may I?"*

"Yes, go on."

"You see, for the last few months I have been listening to the same story. Did... did you actually leave him at the time of crisis?"

After some moments of silence, she spoke, *"I left behind a note that I was leaving, and I actually went up to the station, but I did not board the train. I came back. I didn't know that so much will happen in between my leaving and coming back."* She sobbed as she mumbled the last words.

"One thing," Roy tried to cheer her up as he said, *"Now, we know why he thinks that you are a maid named Moumita."* He handed some pieces of paper to Riya.

"What are these?" she asked as she looked at them.

"I found these in his cupboard tonight- his writings. It seems that he was writing a story based on some servant girl name Moumita just before his accident. I think this is what has blurred his reality more. And I believe that soon he will remember you as your wife and you won't have to be like this anymore."

"Thank you, professor, you have been very kind." She smiled.

Roy affectionately smiled and said, *"I do have a duty towards my friend, don't I? I just can't turn my back on him when he is amnesic. Moreover, I would like to try another doctor, another treatment, but…"*

"But you and I have already spent everything on his treatment till now, and there is no one else who would help us… not even my family members who didn't even accept us on the first place," Riya completed.

"Till when, do you think, will you keep pretending to be a maid?" Roy raised a brow and asked.

"You heard the doctors, right? We cannot do any such thing which stresses him out. I will have to play along with his imagination till things become a little better. But it's ok; I can wait. I can be non-existent for him till he wakes up to reality. I can be non-existent like a ghost," Riya calmly spoke as she guided Roy out of the door.

Roy walked out in the rain and heaved a sigh. He put aside his umbrella and let the storm drench him. He wondered how long he himself would remain a ghost. He had loved Riya since college days, and he was still doing everything he could for her. But he had never been able to express through words. To her, his love remained and still remains a ghost.

Interview

The market smelled of rogue, filth, sweat, penury and wealth; together they gave the putrid smell of unadulterated busy-human-life. She stood there for a while, amidst all the bargaining and bickering, savoring the stench of survival while trying to figure a way out of the marketplace. She looked at her watch, and anxiety on her face clearly suggested that she was getting late. While all this happened, a distant approaching train blew horn, thus adding rhythm to the ongoing concerto of life. Lucy hurried out of the market and started almost running towards a cab on the other side of the road, a bit careless of the un-shoveled snow on the pavement. Her carelessness, perhaps, was a bigger reason than the snow itself, for she slipped, lost her balance and let fly the file that she had been carefully carrying all this while. The file flung mid air, thus revealing its contents- mostly newspaper cuttings, a few transcripts and a questionnaire. All these pieces of paper, bearing different dates and time, had only one thing in common- a name; a name that was known to everyone mostly because nothing was known about him, and the mystery about him had kept people curious and him, famous. The name was 'Nicholas McMillan'. Twenty three years ago, this name emerged as a small enterprise runner and with time, it succeeded in becoming the name of a tycoon. He had successfully eliminated his rivals by drawing and redrawing them to the point of stalemate till they could bear no more losses. It seemed that this guy had nothing to lose; it seemed as if he just rolled dice, picked up spots and kept gambling. Yet, he had successfully kept himself hidden from the media that time and again looked for ways to peep into the lives of the famous. Twenty three years, and nothing was known about his personal life. And soon the curiosity of people shifted from 'what' to 'why'.

Lucy was a self-made, independent woman. Although she liked to call herself a woman, she was more like a child inside. No matter how tough she was from the outside, all she needed was a prick and she would break. And perhaps this was the reason that she had made herself more than tough from the outside, making it tedious for others to read her. Six years back, she started working as a typist for an old man running a small press. While the old man ranted and grunted all through the day, she kept working her way, learning the ways of life, learning how words changed with people. And she did learn that power was the most important thing in this world; everything else just followed. But power, too, needed the fuel of wealth. So there she was, working up the ladder, gaining power and trying to accumulate wealth.

She had already sacrificed a lot in the pursuit of her dreams. A couple of weeks back, when Jaimie, a guy who she was dating, had proposed to marry her, she had felt the turbulence of ecstasy entwined with sorrow while deciding her answer to the proposal. And exactly after an ephemeral eternity of endless enigmas, her fears had echoed, *"This marriage can never happen. I am struggling everyday in pursuit of my dreams, while all you do is sit in your room and daydream about things getting better."*

"But I am trying to..." Jaimie had meekly tried to respond to Lucy's unexpected answer.

"You are trying to do what?" Lucy had silenced him, *"You have quit three odd jobs in the past seven months. You can't even take responsibility for yourself, Jaimie. How can I expect you to look after me? I am sorry if I am being rude, but I feel sorry for your Mom who is still working hard to make ends meet."*

In all his wild fantasies about this moment of the proposal, even the worst ones, Jaimie had not thought about such an eruption of anguished emotions. With quivering lips, he had asked, *"Does it mean that you don't love me at all?"*

Lucy had left the spot immediately, leaving that question answered, for she knew that she couldn't tell him the truth. Her heart had squeezed out tears and she could almost hear her heart screaming, "Yes... I love you, idiot. Yes, I love you like the clouds romance the earth, but clouds can't be tamed. Someday, I will tell you how much I have loved you, but I have got a lot to do before that."

It had taken her so long to get hold of her current job- a journalist. Like every new, aspiring journalist who wanted to make big on the first day of job, i.e. before reality got the better of them, she too wanted to cover a story on someone famous, and like all others who had failed before, she too had taken a chance and had forwarded a letter requesting an interview with Mr. McMillan. But what differentiated her from others was that perhaps the wind favored her sails. Everyone, who came to know about it, shouted with utter disbelief. For the briefest of moments, everyone treated her no less than the queen herself. And so here she was, paying the cab driver as she got down in front of a stupendous mansion, the glorifying yet gloomy-fying view of which, made the dusk appear a bit darker. She wondered how busy a person could be to find time for an interview only after office hours. She felt the chill of wind drying the beads of nervousness on her forehead and then, with her certain, uncertain steps, she walked in as the gatekeepers swung open the gates and another man guided her with a well-practiced friendly smile. *'So it begins,'* she thought.

The man guided her through a magnificent hallway, which more or less looked like an unfinished museum filled with easily inexplicable pieces of arts, to a study that also apparently served as Mr. McMillan's home office. Though the study was very small when compared to the size of the mansion, going by the collection of the books, it was the largest part of the house. She was asked to wait for a while and was left alone in the abyss of knowledge. This room had one large table and only three chairs to call furniture. The light in the room was not dim, but not very bright either; barely comfortable enough to read and write. An old photo frame rested on the table along with a pile of typed and scribbled papers, an old typewriter and a cigar box. She tried to fathom the persona of her host through these, but went cautious when she heard footsteps approaching. She heard the door creak open behind her and a voice behind her coughed and spoke, *"My apologies for keeping you waiting Miss... Parker, right?"* The voice was too soft for a man of his stature.

"Yes," she spoke, as she stood up, trying to sound as much confident as she could, suppressing the armature inside her, *"Yes sir, it's Lucy Parker. And yes, you did make us wait, me and the whole world."*

He laughed a little, amused at her wit and motioned her to sit down as he himself sat down on a chair on the other side of the table- the boss's chair.

"So?" He started, *"I am sure you have got a hell lot of questions, going by the length of the questionnaire."* He threw a glance on the paper that Lucy was holding in her hand. She precipitously pulled it away, feeling a bit foolish to reveal it before the interview even started.

"Relax," he laughed and said, *"This is my first time, too. And I must tell you that maybe I am more nervous than you are."*

The way he said it, allayed her discomfort a little. Though she expected to find this guy snobbish and grumpy, he turned out to be rather balmy. And the comfort, thus established, eased their communication, and the interview began.

The initial questions were mostly related to his current work, future plans for expansion, charity and competition, questions that he answered with properly weighed words, chosen with languid care that seemed to be intended.

"So where is your business heading now?" she asked.

"Well, right now, at 7:40 pm," he replied as he looked at his watch, *"my office is closed… so no business."*

They laughed and then he gave her the answer with some numbers and figures.

"What about your competitors?"

He looked up, raised his right brow a little and then asked, *"Are you sure they still exist?"*

And again, there were smiles.

"What do you feel about charity?"

"Well, that is the best business, I will say. You see, the number of needy people keeps on increasing, and so does the money going in for charity. But no one questions about where the money is going."

"You are not a very religious person, I believe," she asked, amused by his answer.

"Religion is 'The Business' if you ask me. Millions of people are investing in it every day, trying to wash away their past sins, so that they can make space for the future ones. All you need to do is kneel and pray, and all your sins are gone… whoosh… and you are ready for the new ones. And of course, then there are donations; larger the amount, greater the forgiveness," he sarcastically commented. *"You see, I believe in God. I just find religions funny and discriminatory, dividing people and faith since I don't know how long. Our ancestors, the primitive ones, did not have religion, yet they gave us civilization, and what are we doing with religions? Heading towards another dark age?"*

"Deep," she mumbled, thoughtfully.

Then, they both went silent for a while as a maid walked in with tea and filled their glasses with water.

"So…" Mr. McMillan broke the silence, *"Are you not going to ask me anything about my personal life? How I started? Where is my family? And all those questions, which I am sure, the world is waiting to know answers of?"*

"Actually, I was going to…" Lucy started, but was interrupted

"Actually, these are the questions that I called you here for. It's been a lifetime I am running away from these, but now the answers to these questions daunt me. I wanted to answer these questions when I received your proposal for this interview. I thought the media had forgotten me…"

She smiled, a bit skeptical though now; her uneasiness returned as she saw the uneasiness on her host's face. *"So, Mr. McMillan tell me something about your family, friends and how you started your business."*

He looked up, cleared his throat, loosened the knot of his tie, gulped a glass of water and started, *"My father was a butcher, and he had his meat-shop set up in the downtown. I am sure you don't know anything about that locality. It is filthy and… whatever. I used to spend the time off my school by helping my father deliver meat to the houses of the prominent people, here in uptown. Among these houses was this house, not far from here, where she used to live- Amelie, or Amy as I used to call her."* He looked at the photo frame on the table. *"Her father was a lawyer, a very famous one. Every evening, when I knocked at her door, she would come over her room's window and throw a candy at me. It soon became a game for us, for the kids we were. I still remember the first time she did that. She giggled when she threw a candy at me, and it was awkward for me. I was unsure if I should even pick it up. Actually, I thought that she was trying to bully me like the other uptown kids. And I ran away as soon as I handed over the meat to the butler. This continued to happen for a next few days. She would throw candy and I would run away. This continued till one day when she stopped... and that discomforted me. I would keep waiting, looking at her window, but she won't come. Then, one day, I saw her staring at me from her window; her expressions clearly showed that she was now weary of my unresponsiveness. I removed my cap, waved at her, smiled and gestured her to throw candy. She giggled, turned back and after a few moments, showered me with a lot of candies. I was happily picking them up when the butler opened the door. He took the meat and chided me away in a way I will never forget. While walking out of the gate, I turned back to look at her. She was laughing like the wild wind set free. And thus began this little game of ours while the pendulum kept the clock running and us, aging."* He paused with a smile that faded away as he began again, *"I later stopped going for deliveries and started taking studies more seriously. At this point of time, our friendship had taken the form of a clandestine romance. I must admit that I was not a bad student. I dreamed and I dreamed big. I knew that our togetherness would not be accepted unless I did something big, and I knew that I would do something big. All I needed was some time, but time was something we ran out of,"* he let out a suffocated sigh. *"You see, this world we live in, the people around us, I never understand them. A person's own life itself is a great story, and people are capable of making their stories even better, but still it is the story of others that interests them. Seriously, look around. Why do you think that these fiction story books or these newly started motion pictures are so popular? Our own lives can be much better than the love stories shown on pages or screens, and still, here we are, paying for them nonetheless. Anyways, so here we were, standing like culprits in front of her parents and her neighbors. The neighbors, according to them, had caught us red-handed. Then came the emotions and followed the pain of separation. She wanted to run away with me while we still had some chance. She told me that she had convinced the butler to plan her escape. But I knew that when the time comes, we won't survive on love. Love is necessary, but not enough. I really wanted to take her away with me, but..."* He abruptly stopped.

"But you... just had to leave," Lucy completed with expressions of disbelief on her face.

"It was not as easy for me as you said. I wanted to take her away, but she was like a captive princess guarded by dragons in a castle. Once, I tried to break in, but was caught, thrashed and trashed."

"And you gave up?" Lucy asked.

He got irritated a bit, but he was prepared for this. He continued, *"I promised myself that I would come back and take her with me. My father, who was worried for me, gave me some money, and I was out of this place, looking for a way to earn my way back to her. Initially, I started running errands for small shopkeepers, learning the tricks of trade, maligning my honesty with the lies of business, and thus, I worked towards building my own empire. All this while, I thought only about my Amy. In fact, I thought so much about her that I always felt that she was with me, and I almost forgot that she was waiting for me back here. I forgot that I had to return to her. Four years later, when I returned to this place as a successful gentleman, I directly went up to her house with all those hopes of love bubbling inside. I knew that she would understand; I knew that she would forgive me. I knew that her family won't refuse me anymore, and I was dreaming about all these beautiful things that were about to happen next when I saw a sign outside her house. The sign read 'SOLD'. The door, of course, was locked. I almost got frenzied and started running about the place, and then, a neighbor gave me the news. It was the same neighbor who had caused all the trouble in the first place. She told me…"* He paused and sighed again. *"She told me that Amy was… she… she was expecting a child after I left… my child. Her father was embarrassed… so much… so… that he stopped showing his face to anyone. Amy had given birth to a son. To save face from society and to start afresh, the family had moved out of the place. This is what the neighbor told me. I looked everywhere I could, but I couldn't find them- Amy and my son. I just imagined them happy together. How I wish I could change things. I would run away with her if I could now. Why did I do this to them and myself? I just wanted to be with them. Once, I had everything in nothing, but now, I am left with nothing even when I have everything."* He stopped and stared blankly at Lucy's face.

Lucy lifted up the glass of water and emptied it in a single gulp with the sound of water washing silence down her throat. Then she spoke, *"That is why this interview? Now, you want to reach them so that you can undo all this?"*

"Yes… I… err…"

"Why now? It has been so long as you said." Lucy scribbled something on her notebook.

"I learned from my father that she used to come almost every day asking about me when I was gone, but I, somehow, managed to console myself with a belief that she had married

someone else and was happily living with my son and her new family. Later, I was afraid of facing them and facing the world. I was a coward. It took me these many years to…" He stopped again.

"So… That's the reason you have been away from the media, away from people… and family?"

"She was my family."

"You know how the world is going to react when they read your story in tomorrow's newspaper, right?" She attempted a failed smile.

"I don't give a damn. Thinking about them has stopped me for so long. I just want to ask for forgiveness from Amy and my child. I just want to get back to them… I just…" His voice broke… And he held the photo frame on the table towards her.

"Beautiful," she said as she looked at the old photograph. The fold-lines on the photograph clearly showed that it had travelled a lot in wallets.

"That she is."

Lucy looked at him with sympathy in her eyes, got up as she gathered the papers on which she had been scribbling McMillan's answers and spoke, *"Interview is over, Mr. McMillan… Thank you for your precious time and your revealing answers."*

McMillan guided her outside and insisted on giving her a ride on one of his own cars, but a stubborn that Lucy was, took a cab back home.

———◆———

Next day, as the world awaited newspaper, Mr. McMillan also sat waiting for it to see how ruthlessly had he been bashed with words. He unfolded the newspaper as it arrived. *'I know the contents, but the world would be surprised,'* he thought, but exactly the opposite did happen. His interview story mostly covered his business and work life that the world was mostly aware of. Nowhere was mentioned about his unfateful fate that had led to such a comic tragedy in his life. While he tried to cogitate on the different possibilities that could have resulted in this situation, the butler arrived with an envelope in his hand.

"A man just dropped it at the gate, sir," he said, *"It is addressed to you."*

Mr. McMillan quickly opened the envelope. Inside, there was a letter and another envelope. He unfolded the letter and started reading:

> *Dear Mr. McMillan,*
>
> *There are a few things about your story that even you don't rightly know, I assume. The first being: you never had a son. Amelie Louis Parker gave birth to a daughter named Lucy Louis Parker. Second, it is true that Amelie's family left the town, but what you don't know is that they never took the reason for their shame with them. This reminds me that I do know about how the downtown locality is. I grew up there. That is where Mamma brought me up.*
>
> *Since Mamma won't ever tell me anything about who my father was, I always liked to imagine that you were some kind of a war hero who had lost his way back home. So you*

don't have to carry the guilt for me anymore; I forgot and forgave you long back. As for asking for forgiveness from Mamma, you can visit her at the St Angels Cemetery, where she has been resting in peace for the past twelve years. Now, don't try to reach me. Neither you, nor your wealth interests me.

One last thing: Next month, I am getting married to a guy from downtown.

Lucy Parker

He opened the second envelope and found an old photograph- a little girl holding the hand of a beautiful woman- the woman was no one else but Amy, his Amy, or his not.

Far, in downtown, Lucy cried in Jaimie's arms after she expressed her love to him. There was so much to do, but she did not want to be late for the "more important things" as her father did.

WITHERING

It was early morning. One could even say that it was just a second dawn before the daylight actually came to life. Fog and clouds roamed together over the lake while dew drops romanced the petals of blooming flowers. As the monastery gong sent ripples of peace across the valley, Vasu adjusted his thick glasses, mumbled a prayer and walked into an inn with his bulk of luggage. He had just arrived in the valley.

It took him an hour or so to get rid of the weariness that the journey had greeted him with. Though the innkeeper asked him to stay back and rest for a while, Vasu was already out, roaming around with a small bag that contained his useful bearings.

Vasu made his way towards the marketplace while looking around with an eager happiness. Not many shops were open yet. A few stalls were yawning to the mundane life while others still struggled to crawl out of the autumn slumber. Vasu quietly made his way to a small roadside tea stall and ordered a cup of tea. The stout Nepali guy running the stall seemed to be a very amicable guy. He talked about the history of the place, the native culture and the political situation. He also informed Vasu about all the places that he needed to visit before he left the place. Vasu quietly listened and occasionally acknowledged with smiles.

Clouds were raising curtains now, and a part of the sun was peeking out, glistening like a copper coin. Soon, the street was filled with giggles of kids going to school and smiles of the monks going towards the monastery. Vasu sat with his eyes closed, listening to the valley, listening to its joys, prayers, sorrow and life.

"So, why are you here, sir?" Gurung, the guy running the stall, interrupted his meditation.

"Why do you ask?" Vasu asked back, seeming a bit irritated.

"I am sorry if I disturbed you, sir," Gurung apologetically smiled and meekly said, *"but tourists don't visit us during this time of the year. Only a few journalists and writers visit us during this time,"* he chuckled. *"Are you one of them?"*

"Oh! No," Vasu muttered, *"I used to be a journalist, but right now, I am here because I have been advised by my doctor to visit this place."*

Gurung did not respond to that. He quietly stared at Vasu's face for a while and then got busy with tea preparation.

Vasu's cup of tea was almost over now, and he was just thinking if he should order another cup. As he took the last sip and handed the cup of tea to the Gurung, his eyes caught something... rather someone- A woman in her late twenties or early thirties walking down the street to the marketplace, pushing her way through the crowd towards a bench under a lamp post. Vasu kept staring at her. So beautiful she was, and so mesmerized Vasu was that he didn't even realize that he was spilling tea over his shirt. For a moment, he felt that the beautiful valley itself had incarnated in a woman. He was not even listening to the murmurs around. He just looked at her without even blinking his eyes.

"Who would say that she is blind?" mumbled Gurung as he caught Vasu staring continuously at the woman.

"Blind?" Vasu asked, bewildered, *"Yes, she did get greeted with foolish collisions from the crowd, but the ease with which she is walking as if she is certain about the direction, I was wondering who actually is blind here. Her? Or the crowd?"*

Gurung laughed, *"Good observation, Saab. You see, the problem is that people have also forgotten about her eyesight. And it is only because of the ease with which she walks and her non-dependency on anyone...but..."* he paused.

"But?" asked Vasu, as he motioned for another cup of tea.

"But the reason she does not need anyone for support is that this is the only place she walks down to; from the convent to here, early in the morning, and back to the convent, late in the evening. This is what she has been doing for the past ten years."

"Ten years?" asked Vasu, turning his gaze from the woman to Gurung, surprise was quite evident on his face, *"Ten years, you said Mr...?"*

"Naveen Gurung," he promptly replied, *"You can simply call me Gurung, but if you shout my name a bit loud, almost half of the market will be here, thinking you called them,"* he laughed, waiting for Vasu to join him as well, but seeing Vasu's uninterested face, he continued, *"Well, some say it*

has been seven years that she has been doing so, some say it's ten years, others say even more. Honestly, I am not so sure, but it has been five years, since I set up this stall here, and I have been seeing her ever since. It's the same routine every day; she comes here, sits on the bench and waits, a nurse comes at around 1:00 pm with her lunch and medicines, and then again, she keeps waiting. She waits till around 7:00 in the evening and then, she goes back."

Vasu's expressions became a little serious as his gaze turned towards the woman again.

"Well, you must be thinking that the woman is mad, and maybe she is," Gurung caught Vasu's anxious expressions, *"but what everyone knows here is that this woman… she is a legend… a legend with a legendary love story."*

Vasu promptly turned towards Gurung, asking, *"What story?"*

"Another cup of story… I mean tea?" Gurung motioned towards Vasu's emptied cup.

Vasu smiled and said, *"Only a fool will say no to such good tea."*

Gurung held his head up with pride and handed another cup of tea to Vasu as he began narrating, *"The story started when the political scenario in these terrains was at its worst. Demonstrations, strikes, protests became household words. But these, mostly, were in forms of non-violent methods. Then once, some insurgents, with pleasure, took advantage of the situation and violence broke the silence.*

She, as you can still see from her ailing face, used to be a very beautiful girl, shy, but full of youth, joy and love. But then came, a stranger in the town. Despite the political scenario, tourists have never been able to stop themselves from coming to beautiful places; places like this valley. And as a tourist he came. He saw her beauty, they say, and he fell in love with her. But she was born with one curse- she was blind. Maybe this blindness was the reason that she couldn't see the things to come," Gurung paused with a dramatic gesture, looked at Vasu and then continued, *"Her father was a respectable teacher at the convent, and he was a bit orthodox too. Even he agreed to marry her with this stranger, and they were soon to be betrothed. But one day, while she was waiting for him, they say, right there, sitting on that bench, under that lamp post, some insurgents gave spark to violence. Some form of riot broke out and soon the military was on the ground. She heard the mob fighting, crying and howling. She was too scared to get up and walk away. How could she walk amidst the chaos; she was blind. So, scared, she waited for this stranger. Neglected, amidst all the violence, she just waited. But the stranger never came. Military rescued her to safety, they say. But she won't go; she just wanted to wait for her stranger. When they found her, she was already half mad.*

Some say that the stranger, like a coward, ran away with all the other tourists when he saw the violent situation. Some say that he died along with a few others when the military used open gunfire to suppress the violence, and then, there are others who believe that there never existed any such stranger, that is, this woman here, she has always been delusional. They believe that this lover of hers was a figment of her imagination. No one knows for sure. Her father, too, died after a few days of the violence."

Vasu smiled as he looked at his almost empty cup of tea, *"Strange... She has been waiting really long then."*

"Yes," Gurung replied, *"She took a vow that she would keep waiting. Her stranger or death, whoever comes first, she would go with him."*

"Indeed! Death can be such a spoilsport," Vasu chuckled and then asked, *"What about this man staring at her from a distance. It has been long, I noticed, this person came and he has been continuously staring at this… woman,"* Vasu motioned towards a man sitting on another roadside bench; his eyes were on this woman, *"Who is he?"*

Gurung peeped out, his brows tensed, and then, he spoke, *"Actually, I have been seeing this man for the past two weeks. He always comes after this woman does, and he sits here all day long staring at her. In between, he goes somewhere, but he comes back again."*

"Could he be…" Vasu waited for Gurung to complete.

"I… I mean, we never thought about it… maybe… but then, I don't know."

"Hmm… Ever thought of telling this woman about this man?" Vasu seemed to be amused.

"No… no… I don't think it will be appropriate."

"Thank you, Gurung Daju, both for your cups of tea and sips of stories," Vasu winked as he paid for the tea. Then he turned back and made his way towards the bench where the woman was sitting.

"Wait. Are you going to tell that woman about this man?" screamed Gurung.

"Well, maybe. You never know what may become of her story," Vasu waved goodbye to Gurung as he paced towards the woman.

He stood at a little distance from the woman and looked at the mystery man watching him and the woman. Vasu was not sure from the man's face if he was nervous. He was trying to read his expressions when he heard the woman speak, *"You limp a little when you walk if I am not wrong."*

Vasu chuckled and with a suppressed meek tone and spoke, *"You are not wrong and that idiot told me that you can't..."* he stopped.

"Well, I am blind," she spoke with a smile, *"but that doesn't mean that I can't hear as well."*

"True..." Vasu started but was interrupted.

"I am not done yet. You tried to suppress your footsteps while walking towards me. It means that you were not sure if you should come and talk to me. Talk to me? Definitely, you stopped while approaching me and waited; waited without speaking, and you quietly kept waiting," she paused for a while, *"but while answering, your tone went meek and thus your voice, fake. So tell me, what do you want to say or ask?"*

"I just..."

"Before you ask or say anything stupid, let me make it clear that I don't have the power of foreseeing future as the people around here might have told you. If that is the case, you have just been made a fool out of," she blurted.

"Well I am sorry, but after this, my voice is definitely going to sound more polite and thus more fake," Vasu replied as he stepped towards her and sat on the bench while still maintaining a respectable distance. Then he started, *"Ma'am, I am not very good with words like you are. And so, I will directly ask you what I want to know."*

"Though I think I already know your question, go ahead," a morose smile complemented her melancholic voice.

"That tea stall guy told me that... that you have been waiting for your lover for the past..."

"For the past eleven years," she bluntly completed his statement, *"and you sir, if you have come to me only so that you could amuse yourself on my apparent madness, I request you to leave. I respect your way of madness with life, whatever it is, and I expect the same in return,"* her voice echoed a suppressed rage.

"I swear, ma'am, that I don't intend to hurt you by mocking you," he looked at the man looking at them who was perhaps wiping sweat off his forehead, *"I want to know about that man. How did you meet? How did he look like and…"* there was silence, *"How did you separate?"*

"Why should I tell you, Mister?" she seemed agitated, *"Have you got no one else to pester early in the morning?"*

"Ma'am, to be honest, I have never been a believer in true love. I find it difficult to believe that one can spend so many years waiting for love. And yet, when I see you, my heart betrays my belief."

"What is life but a sum of waiting from one day to another? All we do every day, in one form or the other, is waiting. Some work hard waiting for a golden tomorrow, some lie down and wait for the day to end. Then what harm can waiting for love do? It is all about that lump of flesh in our chest that keeps beating to the rhythm of hope and faith," she calmly said, paused and then began her story, *"It was an early autumn morning and I was sitting on the stairs of the monastery waiting for my father who was offering his prayers inside.*

'Excuse me,' a voice startled me, 'Do you know this address?'
'What address?' I coldly asked.
'The one on this card,' it was the voice of a man… a young man as I understood.

'Read it out. I can't see,' I angrily said as I thought that he was some local folk trying to make fun of my eyesight.

'Oh! I am sorry. I did not know,' he replied.

I heard him stepping back. 'So don't you want to know about the address? Or is it that you think I won't be able to help you just because I am blind?' I asked, agitated.

Before he could reply, my father was back and he asked the man why he was troubling me. He recited him the situation in such a hurried manner that it made me laugh badly. I know it was rude but I simply couldn't hold it back. Father did give him the directions and he did scold me for my behavior. But I somehow felt that the man had looked back at me with a smile while walking away. I don't know why, but I felt something.

A couple of days later, he bumped on to me again. I was out in the market with a friend and I heard him again.

'I am sorry about that day, Miss. How are you doing?' he asked.

I usually don't remember all the voices I hear. But this one, I did. I was startled again and it took me some effort to reply, 'I am good, but actually I should be the one to apologize. I should not have laughed the way I did.'

'You shouldn't. I am glad that I could make you smile and laugh,' he babbled.

The statement alarmed me. I had been told similar things before by the people who pitied me, and so I asked him, 'What do you mean? I don't need your pity.'

'No, no, you got me wrong again,' there was innocence along with guilt in his voice, 'What I meant to say is that I am glad that I could witness such a beautiful smile. I have never seen such a magical thing before.'

I was trying to figure out what he meant, but before I could, he left, saying 'I hope to see you again. I really hope.'

With that, I heard him on his foot… almost running away.

My friend teased me all the way back home and she told him how nervous the guy was.

Next day, I was again at the monastery. As soon as my father left for prayers, I heard him again.

'Hello,' he softly greeted me.

'Were you actually waiting for my father to leave? How long have you been following me?' I teased him.

'Not much, only for the last one hour,' he chuckled.

'And why?' I was so full of questions.

'Because I felt like doing so,' he replied.

Then, there was silence for a prolonged moment. I was not so sure about how I wanted to react and he too was weighing his words perhaps.

'Your father will be here any moment now. I will see you tomorrow again.' He left with that. I wanted to stop him, but he was still a stranger to me.

Soon, it became a routine that we sat and talked in the monastery. There were days when father won't come. And those were the days we would sit and talk for hours. What we talked would never make sense to anyone else. He used to tell me about his work for which he was in the valley, he used to tell me about his orphanage where he grew up, and he used to tell me about his dreams.

Then, one day, he held my hands and said, 'I don't promise you wealth and glory, but I can promise you the freedom to be who you are. I don't promise you happiness forever, for life will be full of troughs and crests, but I can promise you that together we will face everything with a smile. I can't promise you that

I will always be with you, but I can promise you that I will always love you till death parts me from you. Will you, Annie, accept me with these promises?'

You might have already guessed that there was no reason to not accept him. My father, who had been secretly keeping an eye on us, accepted us as well. He was happy to see us happy together. Then one day, when I was waiting for him, here, right at this spot, something terrible happened. I still don't know what and why. I was waiting for him but he did not come. People say terrible things about him. They say that he left me; they said that he died; they even say that I am crazy. But I have faith that he will come back," she stopped with tears rolling down her cheeks.

Silence echoed through the valley. Vasu sat there, looking at her face. He could feel the warmth of tears on his own face as well. Then he turned his gaze towards the mystery man who was now walking towards them with slow steps. The man stopped and looked at Vasu's questioning face and motioned him to come towards him.

"Thank you for your story, ma'am," Vasu said to the woman, *"I hope you meet your stranger soon again."*

He got up and was about to walk towards the man when the woman caught his hand and said, *"Vasu,"* she got up from the bench *"I know it is you. I always knew that you would come back. I would wait for you for another forever if I had to."*

The wind howled through the valley, silencing the two wailing hearts, as Vasu took Annie in embrace and lifted her up in his arms. The wait was over for the two fools.

"Vasu, you promised that we would get married before the autumn was over," whispered Annie as tears choked her throat.

"Yes," Vasu looked around at the withering willows shedding away their glorious leaves and then spoke, *"I guess, the autumn is not over yet."* They held each other while the dry wind tried in vain to steal away their tears. In embrace, they stood, for they knew that the eternity of waiting could be best answered by silence and love. And right now, at this moment, they had both.

Though there were many things Vasu had got to tell her, he decided to remain silent for now. He had to tell her how on the day of the riots he had come out of his lodge and had heard about the ongoing turmoil. Before he could reach the marketplace, someone had hit him on his head. He had felt consciousness seeping out of his body, but he still had crawled towards this place because he knew that she was waiting. He had to take her somewhere safe. So he had kept crawling. He had seen her sitting here on this bench, and only when he was six yards away from her, there was darkness in front of his eyes. He had tried to scream but his voice had gone missing. He had tried to crawl but couldn't. And then, he was in the abyss of dark.

He had opened his eyes in some hospital in the city. Most probably, the military had found his address from the lodge he was staying in, and back they had sent him to the city after preliminary treatment. How would have they known that his heart belonged here?

Yes, he had opened his eyes, but he hadn't come to senses. He had tried to speak, to sit up, to move his arms, but all in vain. *'Coma'* he had faintly heard the term doctors were using for his situation. Eleven years, he had waited… waited to wake up from the never ending sleep, so that he could come back to her. Every single day, he had tried to speak up… speak up about her, so that someone could bring her to him or take him to her, but all in vain.

But the past didn't matter right now. They had a lifetime of togetherness to share these stories. Vasu looked towards the tea stall where Gurung was scratching his head and then, he looked at the man standing two yards away from them. He had stopped walking towards them now and was smiling at him. Vasu smiled back, implying, *'It was all possible because of you, good friend.'*

A month back, when Vasu finally started speaking, and movements started coming back to his body, the first thing he spoke about was his love. His doctor as well as a childhood friend, Rana, promised to help him. And thus, two weeks earlier, he himself came and found her. But he was a little worried when he informed Vasu about her.

"I want you to take it really slowly when you meet her," he had told Vasu.

"Why?" Vasu had asked as he had thought he would simply go and lift her up with joy.

After informing Vasu about her daily routine, Rana had said, *"She has been repeatedly doing the same thing every single day; same routine over and over again. As a doctor, that discomforts me."*

"I don't understand what you say. She can't…"

"I am not saying that she is cognitively impaired, but I am just saying that it is better if we act a bit cautiously. What if she doesn't remember you at all? Don't go and tell her everything straight. Because sometimes when someone is already

comfortable with a marred reality, a new reality affects him or her adversely. You may lose her if that is the case."

"Then?"

"Talk to her, listen to her part of the story and check for factual correctness. See if she speaks the truth, exactly as it happened. Then, slowly reveal yourself when you are sure that she has not... she has not flavored the truth with imagination."

Vasu had been doing the same. He looked at the doctor, Rana, his friend, once more with respect. Rana nodded his head and turned back. He had been too worried since morning. First, for this woman; he was not sure about how she would accept the change; and then, for his friend, Vasu, who he had woken up from a coma after an eternity of treatment and who, he knew, would not be able to sustain any other mental trauma. He was apprehensive about what would happen if she didn't recognize Vasu. *'But then,'* he thought as he looked back at them once more, *'why on earth should anybody be worried for these fools. They are in safe hands of each other.'* He stepped over some dry leaves as the wind rustled over them; he first looked around at the withering autumn trees and then at the two fools embraced and withering in love.

THE REAPER AND THE MONK

For hours, he had been meditating, trying to see the light inside, and then, the Monk slowly opened his eyes to the dark, realizing that it was night already. In an attempt to purge away the darkness, he lit a lamp and looked out of the window. In the fading moonlight, he saw snow freezing the leaves of trees; he saw a million glittering fireballs, up in the sky, that failed to warm up the soul of earth on nights cold like this, and then, he laid his eyes on the darkness which became denser with the woods, reminding him of the austere life he had been living in the wilderness for an eternity now. Twenty-seven years ago, he had chosen the path of light. He had left behind his fortune and mortal cravings for the world and had started living in the woods, alone and aloof from the world. The solitude had brought him closer to the light that he came in search for- the one true light, as he would call it or God, as others would. Not even once had he thought of returning back to the so-called civilization. So, never had he thought of seeing any other human form again. But he saw one, recently.

A couple of days back, while out in the woods in search of food, he had found a man lying wounded and unconscious. Going by his wounds, the Monk was pretty sure that he had been mauled by some wild beast. He had, somehow, managed to drag him to his hut and had nursed him since then. In fact, the Monk had devoted all his time and knowledge in trying to cure this man who had not yet regained consciousness. He wondered how and why this man got so far into this dense forest. But he knew that he would not have to wait for long; the herbs were working their magic and were healing the wounds fast.

His hut had only two rooms- a meditating room and the other where the Monk used to sleep. The Monk, with the lamp in his hand, entered this other room where he was treating the wounded stranger. He entered the room with an intention to inspect his wounds again, but he was taken aback by the presence of a second stranger in the room who was hovering over the wounded man.

"Who are you? What are you doing to this person? And how did you get in?" the Monk asked in a worried, yet calm tone.

The stranger also got startled by the Monk, and he looked around to check if there was a fourth person in the room as well. Then in a quivering tone, he asked, *"Can you see me?"*

"Yes, of course!" the Monk replied, *"Now answer my questions."*

"*Yes, of course you can see me! You seek the true light and thus, nothing in the dark remains hidden from your eyes.*" He chuckled and stood up.

It was then that the Monk saw him properly in the dim light. The man wore a loose white shirt with garters and loose trousers. He wore a black hat which failed to conceal his long black hair. The Monk could not tell the age of this man from his face. In fact, his whole persona was a paradox in itself. He was lean but seemed to be strong. His face was pale and lifeless, but eyes were full of joy and life. He smiled at the Monk and the Monk observed that even his smile was warm, friendly, morose and wicked at the same time. He felt that everything about this person was so innocent and yet so deceptive, tense and yet so serene. His faced looked like that of a very old person, yet his skin seemed to be that of a child. Most importantly, he seemed to absorb all the light from the lamp and gave an impression of darkness, yet again, his visage emanated light. The Monk, never in his life, had even imagined such a person.

The man smiled as he calmly spoke in a booming voice, "*Hello, Monk, answering your first question, I am an agent of nature in a broader sense. Secondly, I was just checking how much life is still left in this injured guy, and as for your third question, sorry I cannot answer that; it's confidential.*" He winked at the Monk.

"*What do you mean by an agent of nature?*" Monk asked curiously.

"*Well,*" the man replied, "*to put it in a right way, I help souls make comfortable and safe passage from this realm to the others.*"

"*Are you Death?*" the Monk asked in a worried tone.

"*Put that light away from my face please,*" pleaded the man and then spoke, "*No, I am not Death. Boss does not come down on the field to work except for severe cases of catastrophes, calamities and wars. I am a mere agent working for him.*"

"*What?*"

The man let out a sigh and spoke, "*Some call me a Reaper; in some places, I am a Duta; for some, I am a rider, and in the place where you come from, they call me a Shinigami, and no, I don't carry a scythe or dress myself in a black cloak. It's too inconvenient travelling that way.*"

The Monk knew what Shinigami meant. "*Death spirits,*" he thought, "*the ones responsible to collect souls at the time of someone's death.*" Petrified, he remained silent for some time and then asked, "*Why are you here?*"

"*I am on duty,*" the Reaper replied with a smile.

Monk threw a glance at the injured guy who was still unconscious and everything became clear to him. "*Death has come upon this poor guy,*" he thought and felt helpless, but he knew that he needed to do something. Trembling though, he said, "*I won't let you take this poor soul.*" He pointed at the injured man.

"*What?*" Reaper asked, baffled by what the Monk said, as if he was not prepared for it. He thoughtfully looked at the man lying down, whose breaths were slowing down with time and then at the Monk who didn't seem to be afraid anymore. Then, he calmly said, "*Humans never cease to amaze me.*" He chuckled and spoke, "*I will of course take him at the opportune moment. But tell me Monk, why would you want to save someone who you don't even know? You found him dying in the forest, if I am not wrong. What has his life or death got to do with yours, Monk?*"

"*You won't understand that. Lurking in the dark has made you blind, Reaper. You won't understand the common soul that humans share, binding each of them and imparting each of them with a duty towards each other, a duty called humanity.*" Monk's voice was firm and calm.

"*Such abhorrence, always...*" Reaper said, trying to hide the pain in his voice. He cleared his throat, took out an hourglass from his pocket, put it on a table near the bed on which the injured person was lying, cleared his throat again and spoke, "*Though my colleagues always say that I should accustom myself with this hatred, but I find it difficult. You are a wise man, Monk. Yet, you say that we are blind to humanity, that we don't have any concern for life. What if I told you that destruction or death is the first step towards creation or life? Old ideas have to die for new ideas to replace them just as a tree withers so that new leaves and flowers can get to see the light. That is how nature works and we just help balancing her. And believe me when I say that Life and Death work together. While I am here to collect a soul, an agent of life is out there helping giving birth to another two. As I said, it does not end here.*"

"*I understand that, but I don't understand how conveniently you take anyone without thinking much about the other lives involved...*" Monk started but was interrupted by Reaper.

"*Conveniently? Without thinking?*" Reaper looked at him with surprise.

The Monk ignored his surprise and continued, "*Twenty-seven years ago, you took my beloved wife from me. I am not complaining. I am far beyond the virtual realities of the world, but I won't let you take another life when I can stop you. This man, here, must be having a family to return to and unfinished works to complete.*"

The Reaper, dumbfounded, looked at the Monk for a while and said, "*I want to tell you a story, Monk- an ancient fable.*" He looked at the hourglass through which the sand grains were pouring faster now and then started, "*Once, a mother, upon death of her six years old child, decided to follow Death to his realm and get her son back. And so she started tracing Death to his kingdom. I won't go into the details of her sufferings throughout her journey, but what I can tell you is that she did reach the realm of Death and of course, in a very bad condition- wounded, bleeding, delusional. I will tell you what happened when she reached our realm. Unexpectedly, she was given a very warm welcome. Everyone was surprised because she was the only mortal who had stepped into that place. She cried and asked the Lord of Death to return back her son, and Death's heart grieved to see all the sufferings she had gone through. He felt helpless; he wanted to help her. But he did something unexpected. He showed her the future of her son if he lived his life. Believe me, it was no trick; the future was an honest future. He showed the woman the sufferings, the pain and the solitary life that her son was destined to live, in case he lived. Then, he showed her where her child was after death and how happy he was. He promised that he would return him if she still wanted him back. She didn't take him back with her. Instead, she asked Death to take her life and reunite him with his son. He, though, did not do any such thing. He healed her wounds; he took the pain of her sufferings and he himself guided her back home. He promised her that he would come and take her when it was the right time. The woman lived a long life and gave birth to another son who became a great leader. Death kept his promise and reunited her with her son when she had completed the great tasks she was destined to do.*

They say that the woman died with a smile on her face." He looked at the hourglass again and continued, *"And if you are still thinking that Death just deceived her by showing her an illusion, Death doesn't deceive anyone even when life sometimes does."* He paused and looked at the Monk, then he spoke again, *"Do you think it's very easy for us to take someone away? It's not. I have seen wars and plagues, and believe me, I have shed tears for all the victims, but I know only one thing: an actor has to leave the stage after he has played his role. There are times when even I don't understand why someone has to die, but 'why' and 'how' are questions beyond my pay-grade. I am given answers to only two questions- 'who' and 'when'. But I know and I believe that life and death have plans for everyone. It's written: your fate."*

Monk remained silent for a while and then spoke, *"Maybe what you said is actually true, and maybe you sometimes guide people to a better place, but still, I am not letting you take this man."*

"*What?*" asked the Reaper, seeming amused.

"*You heard me. Take me instead. I don't fear you."* The Monk said, looking at the hourglass; they were running out of time.

"*First, there is nothing to fear if you have not wronged anyone in your life and second, I will definitely take you… but at the opportune moment."* Reaper innocently smiled.

The Monk felt helpless. He looked at the table on which there were herbs he had used to treat this man, the scissors he had used to clean his wounds, the blood clotted clothes he had washed his wounds with, the bowl of brew he had tried to feed him with, and then, he again looked at the hourglass. He had been treating this guy for long but…

He saw the guy making movements as if he was coming back to life, struggling hard to open his eyes. "Unfortunately," he thought, "he will open his eyes to death if I don't save him."

With quick movements, he picked up the hourglass from the table and smashed it on the floor, breaking it into pieces.

The Reaper looked at him with disbelief in his eyes. *"Breaking the hourglass won't help. That only helps me to keep track of time. Why are you doing this when actually..."* he started mumbling, but was interrupted by the Monk.

"Maybe," spoke the Monk, *"But getting rid of you will definitely save his life."*

Monk held the lamp high towards the Reaper's face.

"Stop it," the Reaper pleaded.

Then, the Monk raised his voice as he started commanding the Reaper, *"In the name of The One True Light, the light of knowledge and wisdom, the light that purges all the evil and darkness, the light that gives us life, I command you to leave this place now."*

"Stop it, Monk," the Reaper kept pleading. The discomfort on his face was evident. He started stepping back towards the window.

"I command you to leave," the Monk kept repeating, cornering the Reaper.

Then, with a bright flash of light, the Reaper vanished into thin air. Monk stood there for some time, dumbfounded. He felt a little weak and exhausted. He was about to turn back when he felt something sharp against his abdomen.

"Where am I?" a coarse voice asked.

The Monk tried to turn his head and see who it was. In the dim light, to his horror, he saw the man he had found wounded in the woods; it was the man he had been nursing all this while. The man was holding scissors in his hands, pointed against the Monk's guts.

Feeling the pain of the metal being impaled into his body, he spoke, "*Western woods.*"

"*I heard you talking to someone. Who else is here?*" asked the man.

The Monk did not reply.

"*Did you inform the cops about me? Who else knows that I am here?*" the voice echoed again.

"*Except death, no one,*" answered Monk.

"*Except death?*" snorted the stranger, "*Are you trying to threaten me?*" He penetrated the scissors deeper into the Monk's body and with a thrust, ripped apart his guts.

The Monk didn't feel pain anymore. He saw a light and in this light, he saw the Reaper at the door, smiling at him. His smile was sad yet warm.

"*I am sorry, Monk. I was not allowed to tell you, but I came for you. You played your part beautifully, and now, it's time for you to see the light, the light you have been trying to see all through your life. Let's go,*" Reaper was speaking to him. "*As for this maniac,*" he said as he pointed at the man who was limping out of the door, passing through the Reaper as if oblivious of his presence, "*he still has to help me with a few more souls. Then, I will give him a gruesome end. Let's go now.*"

The Monk closed his eyes. His face looked pacified, as if he was going deep into a dream. For a moment, he thought that he was seeing the agents of life helping a flower bloom as the world yawned with the dawn. Then, he saw nothing but light, a light that absorbed him and his mortal sufferings.

PORTRAYED

My 14 years old daughter is mad at me. That is not a very rare thing. Often, we, parents of my age and kids of hers, rush into collisions of thoughts and ideas. And of course, we have all the rights to chide them in the process of parenting them because most of the times, their demands are not justified. But my daughter's reason to be angry with me is not wrong. Diya, my daughter, is an artist; a very good one, I must admit. At least, that is what I have heard people saying. But despite the fact that Diya paints well, I have never ever seen any of her works. She wanted me to take her to an art exhibition happening this weekend, but I denied. I told her to go alone or take her mother along with her. And that is what has made her really really angry. It is not that I am against art. In fact, it was me who convinced Diya's mother to let Diya join sketching classes. It's just that I am Sportaldislexicartaphobic. In human words, I am afraid of paintings. But it was not always like this. I myself used to sketch a little bit in my youthful days; actually, a little more than a little bit. But then something happened that replaced my love for art with fear. I will tell you how it happened, but before that, I must tell you that you have all the rights to judge me, but I will use my right to write to write the right- the truth, exactly as it happened.

It was 1977 when I came to Kolkata; oh, it was Calcutta back then. I came to the city looking for a job. And later that year, I found one in the form of a writer for a cheap local magazine. All my educational qualifications put together could not help me get a right job; such was the sociopolitical and economic condition of Calcutta at that point of time. To add to that, my parents did not want me to leave Bengal, for they feared that other states were in an even worse condition. So, I took up the job even though they paid me a meager sum of pennies for all the grey cells I drenched out in sweat. It was that time when I met Bankim Babu. I was looking for a place I could afford, and Bankim Babu was looking for a tenant. He was a very amicable person, and soon, I found myself in a spacious room on Chowringhee lane. My room was on the ground floor, while Bankim Babu had his rooms on the first. A bank clerk by occupation, but a curator by hobby, he had inherited a grand fortune from his father and forefathers who had ruled the place as *Zamindaars* for ages. And to my surprise, he used all this wealth to buy precious junks that he very fondly called antiques, or 'aenteeks' as he used to pronounce the word. This obsession to collect antiques had not only burned a hole in his pocket, but had also left its mark on his personal life. It had led to a debacle of his marriage. A neighbor once told me that Bankim

Babu's wife had left him within four months of marriage, but I never got the courage to discuss this with him. Why would I? He was a nice gentleman offering me a very nice room at a very affordable rental rate when I did not have much to spend. Even Bankim Babu never mentioned his wife or his marriage. He seemed to be happy with his own weird hobby. Now that I am married, I don't wonder why.

Most of my evenings would be spent in Bankim Babu's study, where he would discuss one new antique every day. One day, he would show me an exquisite piece of trinket carved out of silver and another, a broken spittoon made out of ivory. Seriously, I still wonder why anyone would make a spittoon out of ivory on the first place; let alone buy it. Or why would anyone buy a broken watch for thousands when it won't even correctly show the time? And I would like to remind you that I am talking about the time when even one hundred rupees was considered to be a great deal of money.

His study was filled with all sorts of weird collections. In a large, glass framed cupboard, which occupied almost half of his room, he had carefully decorated all his 'aenteeks'. The other half of the room was occupied by a large oak table and a couple of chairs. He had told me that even these were antiques. So, I would take extreme care while sitting on these chairs. Sometimes, sitting on these chairs would make me feel uncomfortably glad to think that some Nobles had dined sitting on them. Bankim Babu would often complain that his room did not have much space to accommodate more collectibles. Also, he would get upset upon seeing the empty walls of his room. I would stare and smile at him whenever he told me about his worries because of such misfortunes.

It was February of 1980, and I was enjoying a sip of my favorite Darjeeling tea when I heard some commotion near the main entrance of the building. I scurried towards the gate and saw Bankim Babu shouting at few boys who were trying to lift something very heavy, packed in rags, *"You morons! Can't you be a little careful with that? I spent my forefathers' fortune on that thing. Don't you dare break it."*

I am not a very interfering sort of a person by nature. So I came back to my room, shut the door and sulked at my own sufferings. Later, that evening, Bankim Babu came to my room and took me upstairs to his study.

"Ah! You see, Pratul, I never told you this, but I have been a little upset about the empty walls of my room," he spoke as he guided me upstairs.

"Never told me?" I thought, remembering all those torturous hours of cribbing and complaining. But I rather managed a smile and asked, *"Really? So what are you going to do about it?"*

"You will see," he replied with an enthusiasm equivalent to that of a child eager to show his new toy. And then, we walked into his study.

"What do you think of this?" He asked as he unveiled a large, beautiful mirror placed by the wall by the side of his table. *"Isn't this a piece of sheer beauty. It has travelled all the away from Africa."* He sat on a chair as he fueled his pipe with tobacco.

I must admit that the mirror was extraordinary. I found it unworldly; black metal frame with exquisite artwork and ciphered engravings. It was actually beautiful except for the stained corners of the glass. But even the stains were so symmetrical that they looked like some kind of tattooed pattern.

I was admiring the beauty of the mirror when a reflection on the mirror caught my eye.

"I never saw that before," I said as I turned back and pointed at a painting hanging on the wall opposite to the mirror.

"Yes," Bankim Babu spoke as he made an attempt to light his pipe, *"that painting, they gave as a compliment at a very cheap price for buying this mirror at such a high price. I always keep complaining that they don't give discounts to their most loyal customer. So, this time, the fools offered me one."* He coughed as he let out a cloud of smoke, and then, with a mischievous smile, he asked, *"Beautiful painting, right? It is a good bargain I struck."*

"I thought you bought it in some auction."

"No, I bought this from the antique shop at Dharmatala. I am a regular customer there."

"So who is this?" I enquired as I walked towards the painting with an intention to inspect it.

"Some Philip something Junior, some King or Duke, I am not very sure. They told me," he spoke with pauses, trying to remember, *"but I don't remember. In any case, how does it matter? It is a beautiful portrait, decorating the wall of my room. People just appreciate such art, they don't enquire about them."*

"Yeah, of course." I tried to read the features of the portrait thoroughly, given my own interest in art. This Philip 'something' Junior seemed to be a very mysterious person to me- Bald, slanting forehead, scheming eyes, sly smile and a crooked nose with a big black dot that seemed

to be a mole. The person must have been a little stout in his life. There was something about his eyes, something so cruel that I had to immediately look away. Even the thought of presence of this painting in the room made me feel uncomfortable. After a small discussion about Bankim Babu's next week's auction plans, I left the study, disturbed by the portrait.

A couple of weeks later, I remember, I had just come back from my office. I saw Bankim Babu sitting out in the verandah as I opened the gate to get in. I greeted him, and I too pulled a chair to sit. He raised his cup of tea in a manner someone raises a toast and said, *"Bonjour Monsieur Pratul."*

I must, at this point, inform you that Bankim Babu was not a very educated person. Hence, I was startled by his French greeting. His words were clear and his pronunciation, flawless. After keeping quiet for a while, I asked, *"I didn't know that you knew French?"*

Bankim Babu took his eyes off from the newspaper and asked me back, *"French? I don't know French."*

"But you just spoke to me in French." I thought that maybe he had just learned the words without knowing their origin.

"When? I only said 'Hello' to you. I said 'Hello, Pratul'," he calmly said. He, then, looked at me with concern and asked, *"Are you alright Pratul? You look like you are in trouble."*

Though I was absolutely sure about what I had heard, I decided to keep quiet. Moreover, I was actually in trouble at that point of time. I was getting desperate for a new and a better job. So, we did not discuss about his French anymore and got busy with discussing jobs. He promised me to refer for a better job through a friend of his.

Three days later, I was in my room. Kinkar, the house servant, came to my room and gave me a job recommendation letter. I happily accepted it, shut the door and started reading it. Bankim Babu's flawed English and funny grammatical mistakes made me laugh. But my worries regarding finding a better job assuaged a little. I gladly read it again and again, and I decided to meet this friend of Bankim Babu the very next day. I was about to keep the letter back in its envelope when something caught my eyes- the signature. The letter had definitely been written by Bankim Babu, but the signature was someone else's. In clear, old fonts, the letter was signed by the name of *'Philip Ellington Jr.'*

I rushed to Bankim Babu's study. I did not even think it necessary to knock and ask for his permission to enter the room as I barged in.

"Bankim Babu, you did not sign the letter..." I started but could not complete as I saw Bankim Babu staring continuously at the portrait on the wall.

"Bankim Babu," I called again. This time he responded. He quickly turned towards me, realizing my presence, and said, *"Oh! When did you come? I am sorry, I was a bit lost."*

"What happened?" I asked with concern as I sat on a chair.

"Nothing too serious, I believe. Tell me, you got the recommendation letter I sent, right?" He again threw a glance at the portrait.

"Yes, of course," I replied, *"but it has not been signed correctly."*

"Really?" he asked in a curious tone. *"I thought I signed it properly. Let me see it."*

I handed him the letter and he looked at it for a while until he realized the mistake, and then, his eyes went wide.

"I think I signed it a bit lost-mindedly. I will send you another one in a while," he stammered with an apologetic smile and crumpled the letter.

"That is alright, Bankim Babu, but is everything fine with you?" I asked.

"Yes," he replied as he looked back at the portrait, *"there is nothing to be worried about. It's stupid that I am even thinking about it."*

"What is it?" I asked out of the growing curiosity.

He looked at my face for a while, perhaps deciding if he could trust me, and then, he said, *"This morning, I was combing my hair in this mirror."* He paused to look at his beautiful antique mirror and then continued, *"It was then that I saw the reflection of this portrait on it."* He paused again for a while. Then, with a sheepish smile, he said, *"As I already said, it's stupid, but I saw in the mirror… I felt like I saw that the man in the portrait walking out of the portrait, walking towards me. I stood watching it, mesmerized. I could see his hands out in the air, trying to reach me. Thanks to Kinkar that he knocked the door just then. I felt like I was under some kind of hypnosis and the noise got me out of it. Then, it was normal. I turned back and saw the portrait. It hung there, lifeless, as it always has been."*

He stopped and waited for my reaction, but I was too scared to give any. The mere thought of that sly little man walking out of the painting sent shivers down my spine.

"Maybe that is the reason I signed your letter wrong. My mind was too occupied to think something else." He smiled again.

"*Why don't you take that portrait down?*" I asked, no more able to keep my feelings suppressed.

"*What? But Why?*" he asked, "*Oh! Come on. I just hallucinated. I am not getting enough sleep these days. These things keep happening. Why blame a harmless painting?*"

I wished that he was right about hallucinating, but I still wanted an answer to how could he sign with a name that he didn't even remember, that too, in a handwriting belonging to an entirely different era. But I decided to keep quiet, hoping that it was all because of a mere hallucination.

Days went by, and I, finally, had a new job as a writer for a prestigious daily. Bankim Babu's reference had worked its magic, and I was very grateful to him for the same. He seemed to be rather busy recently. Most of the time, he would shut himself in his study. That was the reason that I had not been able to thank him properly. One day, I remember, I was coming down from the terrace after finishing my *bidi*, and I decided to stop by his study and thank him for the job. He opened the door, but I could not recognize him for moments. It seemed as if he had lost a lot of hair in the past few days. His face, too, was also looking different. He offered me a chair to sit and we started talking, but I was distracted by the change in his face. The innocence in his big, round eyes had been replaced by a plotting, scheming gaze. His smile seemed to be sly. I quickly stole a glance at the portrait on the wall. To my surprise, the face in the portrait seemed to be more familiar to me- innocent eyes, warm smile and hair sprouting on the head.

I quietly sat there, horrified, while Bankim Babu still kept talking to me about his new collections. I knew, for sure, that the portrait was haunted. I knew that I had to get rid of it. I wanted to tell Bankim Babu, but I knew that he won't listen. Then, I thought that maybe I was thinking too much about it. Maybe my mind was playing tricks on me. So, I decided to wait and then take action.

I did not have to wait for long. That night, around 2:00 am, I woke up with a loud noise of someone banging on my door. It was Kinkar. He told me that Bankim Babu was missing.

"I heard some noise from his study. I thought that it may be a thief. So, I decided to wake up Babu first. I went to his bedroom, but he was not there. The door was open. So I took a lathi (bamboo-stick) and went to his study. The door was not locked from inside. As I creaked opened the door, I saw a stranger- a foreigner sitting on Babu's chair. I asked him who he was and he started abusing me in some foreign language. Then, he stood up and took out a sword to kill me. But he was weak. I hit him hard on his head with my lathi. He is unconscious now, I hope, lying on the floor," Kinkar proudly summarized the situation in one breath, *"but I wonder where Babu went."*

I ran upstairs, alarmed by my instincts. Kinkar followed me. I saw the stranger in medieval European clothes lying unconscious. I had seen him before but in a portrait- bald, slanting forehead, scheming eyes, sly smile and a crooked nose with a big mole on it. My eyes, in a reflex, went to the portrait on the wall. It had now become a flawless portrait of Bankim Babu. I don't know why I did it, but I asked Kinkar to immediately take down the portrait and get rid of it. Kinkar stood there with disbelief in his eyes. He had no idea of what was going and why was I asking him to get rid of a portrait when I should have searched for his employer. I wondered how Kinkar missed to see the happenings.

The changes had been taking place for so long. Then I remembered that Kinkar did not used to see Bankim Babu much in his study. Even if he did, his eyes would be on the ground, taking orders or picking up cups.

"*Now*," I commanded him.

He quickly obeyed and called for another servant to help him. It took them a while to lift the heavy portrait and take it out of the room.

As soon as the painting went out of the room, I could hear Bankim Babu coughing and breathing heavily. His face seemed to be changing back to normal, how it had actually been. I could see hair on his head now. I quickly called for an ambulance and took him to hospital.

Bankim Babu was admitted in the hospital for four days. I was there when he regained his consciousness. He drew me near and whispered, "*Pratul, I was amidst a terrifying nightmare. I felt like I was trapped in a painting hanging on the wall. I could see and understand what was going around, but I was helpless. It was agonizing.*"

After getting discharged and coming back home, he did not even ask what happened to the painting. To be honest, even I did not know. Kinkar had told me that he had thrown it away. But Bankim Babu simply felt glad.

Few more days passed. I had now decided to shift to a new apartment by the coming week. I was not very comfortable living with antiques anymore. One day, I remember, I was sitting in the verandah, sipping tea while smiling at my writings in a daily newspaper column. My smiles were, though, soon interrupted by a stranger's voice, "*Are you Bankimchandra Mitra?*"

I looked up at the man who, according to me, definitely did not belong to this country or rather this world. He was a fair looking guy with white hair, beard and moustache. He had kind features and even kinder eyes. His warm smile sent very positive vibes.

"No… No, I am his tenant, Pratul Ray," I answered as I offered him a seat but he refused.

"Please tell Mr. Bankim that I want to meet him. He possesses something that belongs to me, something that was stolen from me."

"Oh! It must be some antique, I believe," I stammered as I stood up with an intention to guide him upstairs to Bankim Babu's study, *"Follow me. He must be in his study."*

As silence followed, he followed me upstairs. I knocked the door twice or thrice, but no one responded. The stranger smiled at me and said, *"Let me try."*

He held the knob of the door and gently turned it. To my surprise, the door, supposedly locked from inside, effortlessly creaked and opened. However, Bankim Babu was not inside. The stranger quietly made his way towards the end of the room without even looking at the valuables in the room.

"I will go find Bankim Babu," I broke the silence.

"That won't happen, I think," he said in a very amused tone.

"No, he must be in his room," I began, but could not finish as I watched what he did.

He silently walked up to the mirror, touched it and whispered, *"Hello there! We meet again. You can't always elude me."*

I too went and stood by his side, wondering what he was up to. At that very moment, a pigeon fluttered over me, almost scaring me to death and flew out of the room. I was wondering how the pigeon got into this room when I heard him speaking, *"This is The Cursed Mirror of Calhoujhezinat, also known as The Moon Mirror or The Muertika. The world is but only a reflection for it, and it loves to play tricks with its reflections- the alive and the dead alike. It is known for its deadly illusions."* He paused and looked at me. *"I am sorry for being late, but you won't find Mr. Bankim in his room anymore."*

I was trying to comprehend what was going on. It was then that my eyes caught something on the mirror, a painting on the opposite wall. I quickly turned back and looked at it. It was a new painting. Bankim Babu must have had put it up recently- a beautiful, serene painting of birds breaking free from all the cages... except for one. In that cage, there was no bird, but a man- a man with a face so familiar that it froze my blood- Bankim Babu.

I turned back to look at the mirror. My own reflection in the mirror was mocking me with hollow eyes and a sly smile. The stranger quickly took out a black veil, which I wondered where he had kept, and covered the mirror. *"I am sorry."* was what I heard the stranger saying before I fainted.

I opened my eyes in a hospital where police was already sitting to inquire about my missing landlord. Kinkar told me that he had not seen any stranger entering or leaving the house. He also told me that the mirror and the painting on the wall, both were missing. Police had got nothing on me and thus set me free, but I could not set myself free from the fear.

This is the reason I am Sportaldislexicartaphobic. Tell me how can I go and visit an art exhibition? Sometimes, I see pigeons sitting on my window, and I wonder what happened to Bankim Babu... Oh! I forgot to mention one more thing; I am Catoptrophobic as well- that is, now, I am extremely afraid of mirrors as well.

FATE OF CLAY

Humans, they say, are nothing but moldings of clay. They rise, easily getting shaped by what they go through, what they hear and what they say; they survive, easily getting corrupted by the emotions of love, lust and hate, time and again; they fall, easily becoming the dust, which they are, leaving behind it all. Easily, the winds of time storm them away and easily, they become stories with their souls scattered over words- words that speak of their glories and words which speak of their fates.

He carefully pushed his way through the crowd, warily hiding his face under a hood. He was cautious enough not to scare anyone and careful enough not to get scared. Then he stopped under a shed from where the castle gates could easily be seen, and he watched the handsome young knight talking to his beast while the people around him bowed and greeted him. He sighed, turned back and walked away.

The knight patted his horse, trying to calm down the beast that seemed to have sensed the upcoming turmoil. A band of soldiers saluted him as they marched past him, reminding him of the commandeering position that he held, reminding him of his duties. There was a huge rush and commotion all around, but the knight looked beyond the noise.

She silently watched the river play with the sunrays as she strolled along the river banks. A nightingale occasionally cooed from somewhere not so far away while the wind howled through the woods and the river sang the glory of its journey. And then, she heard chaos. At a distance, someone blew a conch, and with that, began the rhythmic beat of chaotic drums- war-drums. Its rhythm disturbed the tranquility that she had been enjoying all this while.

The knight got down from his steed as he walked across the golden fields, towards the river banks. He gazed up at the sky where the clouds sheltered the sun that was pouring out its gold; only a part of its corona was visible which appeared to be a great crown. His eyes then caught the shimmering waters of the river as he walked towards its banks and then, finally, he saw her. Her golden hair played with the tunes of the wind while a single lock of hair was caressing her red cheeks. *'No gold in this world can compare with the plethora of gold that my eyes, right now, behold, and yet...'* he thought.

And as if she heard his thoughts, she turned back and looked at him, trying to bring a faint smile on her face, but it only helped her tears find their way out. In silence, they stood for a while, staring at each other like fools, for fools they were- fools of love, of course. And the silence sang the story of their love- the story which only they could hear and love which only they felt.

"*War, is it?*" she broke her silence with a question, the answer of which she already knew.

"*Soulmate,*" he said, as he help up her face.

He had always called her *'Soulmate'*. She was Thea for everyone else, but for him, his love- his Soulmate.

"*I am leaving today,*" he spoke, armoring his heart, for a warrior he was.

"*Leaving?*" she stared at him and said, "*Love dies when men fight; only broken hearts are left behind. Every time that sword of yours rises to protect someone, is wounded by your sword to death, some poor soul's love. I know that it is your duty to fight in the war, failing which would cripple you and make you a coward, yet my selfish heart fears to let you go. I fear what would happen if you go astray too far.*"

"*I agree with you that I kill so that I can protect my own people. But maybe, that is the only way I can defend my share of love- love for my land, people and you. My Soulmate, you don't have to fear anything. I promise I will return and I promise I will return soon,*" the Knight replied.

"*Very well, if you have to go, then may the stars be your guide on the roads and fair winds may sail your boat. I will wait for you right here, every day, till you come back home,*" she spoke to him as she tied a thick black thread around his neck, apparently meant to keep him from harm's way.

Silence, being the purest of all other languages, again found its place between them. Though his unspoken love was not unheard, beneath his armor, felt unsafe, his heart. A flock of birds took flight across the sky, and in an embrace, stood the maiden and the knight... for a while. Then, it was the time to separate. At a distance, blew again, the 'calling for arms' conches and with that, the ugly beats of drums. The knight wiped tears off her eyes and with a kiss, he bid goodbye. Uncertain of tomorrow, they were, uncertain of their fates; unaware of the shadow, they were- the shadow who was watching them.

From behind the bushes, he sighed as he watched her cry; Thea was her name, he had known all the while. He watched her cry as her young knight walked away. Tempted, he was; tempted to go to her and make her smile, but he already knew the consequences. '*I will, again, be the cause of her fright,*' he thought, '*After all, I am nothing but a monster.*'

They called him '*The Monster of the Hills*'. Fools didn't even know that this monster was more human than they were.

He was born a human... like all of them, but with one curse- a deformed face. And ugliness is what they don't accept. At the time of his birth, his mother had thought that she had given birth to a monster. His father had thought that this child was a progeny of his previous life's sins and that the child foreboded more evil.

In a dark basement, they used to keep the child so that no one up in the light could see their shame. All day long, the child would cry in the dark; perhaps light was all he needed, but they would feed him, clothe him and keep him closed inside. As the child started growing up, he started growing restless- restless to see beyond the dark he had always seen. He would often try to run away whenever the basement door opened and he would scream and cry at a pitch of voice that shattered every glass in the house. His parents, soon, started thinking that the child, the monster, was beyond their control.

One morning, when the child woke up, he found the basement door open. Afraid, he was, but not of walking into light (because that is what he had always wanted); he was afraid that he would get scolded again. So, he called out for them and waited for their reply, but the reply never came. He walked upstairs and saw light for the first time. The light hurt his eyes, blinding him with joy- joy of knowing that the world was more than just black. He cried, rejoiced and again, called out for his parents to share his new-found joy. But where were they? It took him a while to notice their absence, and then, he cried out of fear, not joy. He ran berserk in the house, trying to find them. He cried and screamed out a promise to forever stay in the basement, only if they came back. And soon, was gone the light, with hunger, was exhausted, the child. Though darkness was all he had seen in his life, he was still appalled to see the night. Afraid, he was, to walk out of the house; scared, he was, to stay inside. The child cried till his eyes went dry, and then, the dreams took over.

After several days of waiting inside, feeding on whatever he could find, he realized that no one was coming back to him. It was then that he decided to go out in the light and kiss the world with his eyes.

He couldn't understand why people on the road screamed and ran away in fright when they saw him; he thought, '*What causes them plight?*'

The baker gave him bread for free before he was on his heels; the old lady left her pitcher behind to quench his thirst. Strange seemed everything that happened to him, but he enjoyed every moment of being in the light. He giggled, chuckled and danced till he heard the noise of the mob as dusk began.

"*Monster,*" they shouted, "*Let us get rid of this abhorrent creature.*"

He waited, trying to understand who they were talking about. Then a man came forward; perhaps he was some priest. With a loud voice, he commanded, "*Go back to your abeyance, devil.*"

'*Do they mean the basement?*' he wondered. Before he could ask the same, sticks and stones were all over him, and there he lay in the gutters after a while, groaning at the stars for there was no one else to hear. Thus began, his new life; from a child to a monster in a single night.

Initially, he used to come out into the streets only during the night, covering his face. He used to earn his bread by begging. Then, slowly, he started learning the ways of the lives of the so called humans. Occasionally, someone would faint if, by mistake, he revealed his face and then he would have to run away, remaining hungry for the day. He, then, started doing odd jobs for tinkers and blacksmiths, carefully covering his face. Intelligent, he was and soon, he learned many things; from craftsmanship to tinkering to blacksmithing. But most importantly, he learnt one thing that people would not accept his beautiful works if they saw their ugly creator. '*Is being ugly,*' he would often think, '*the greatest sin in this world? Maybe yes. For a good looking person may tell you many lies and still he is forgiven, but even if an ugly one like me speaks the truth, they look at him as if he has lied. They shun an ugly person as if they are different from them. If that is what a human is like, maybe it is better to be a monster.*'

Soon, he started working on his own. All he needed now was a place, a place where he would not have to hide while working. And then, he turned his gaze towards the hills that silently stood towards the eastern end of the city. No one would scare him there. Thus, he created his realm on the hill-top, which also served as his workshop where he spent all his day, creating and inventing. He filled the place with books, inventions and his imagination. He would come down to the city streets only when it was night, carefully clad in a hood. He would sell his work, make his purchase, buy food and distribute food to the street-feds, and then again, he would climb back to his little palace. Occasionally, he would make toys that could not be compared with any other in the world, and on nights, silent and undisturbed, he would leave them on the doorsteps of the city people- people who would find themselves marveling at the unworldly toys, sure enough that the toys were delivered by some angel. But as for our monster, he would just imagine the children playing with his toys and that would be enough to make him smile. Happily, he lived the life of an abject.

Some people had seen him as a shadow, walking up and down the hill, and they had labeled him as 'The Monster of the Hills'. He did not mind; he did not mind till one night. That night, he was out on the streets, making his regular transaction of goods. There, he had seen her for the first time. She was walking across the marketplace- a fair, fair maiden she was. Her locks were teasing her face, and for a moment, he had feared that they would cut her red cheeks. For the first time, he had felt the urge to become humanlike.

They say that falling in love is easy; it is not falling in love that is actually tough; one needs to be tough on his heart for that. And perhaps, he had been tough on himself for too long. He had followed her through the streets; he had followed her to her manor, and he had felt like stopping her and talking to her. But then, he was a monster.

That night had been a sleepless night for him. And the next day, for the first time in an aeon, he had come down to the city during the morning time and had waited outside her manor. '*Maybe,*' he had thought, '*she would accept me as I am. Only once, if she gives me a chance, I would show her what I am inside… Maybe…*'

He had waited till the maiden came outside. He, in his awkward manner, had walked towards her and she, with all her curiosity, had looked at him. Just then, his fate had intruded. A disconcerting wind had blown away his hood, revealing his deformed face and the young maiden had screamed in fright before she fainted. He had run towards her to hold her before she hit the ground. Then, he had heard someone scream, "*Look, the hill-monster has killed her*". Then, he had heard the crowd again. Scared, he had left the maiden behind and had run for his life.

His human heart had ached and yearned for the long forgotten love. He had cried, had mourned, had wailed, but nothing did help. He, now, knew that she would not love him. He was a monster, wasn't he?

There is only one prerequisite to fall in love- do not be ugly. Then why do ugly people have hearts? Why can't they stay away from love? Why don't people kill them young if they can't be accepted? Why are they so different from others? No one answers these 'Why's'… because everyone is busy appreciating the beauty of the world. Who thinks about the 'ugly'? Let them deal with their curse on their own.

He would quietly follow her and watch her from a distance. He knew that he couldn't have her; maybe he could only worship her from a distance. Every day, he would run from one place to another and locate his fair maiden, Thea was her name. Then, one day, he found out that Thea loved someone else. Though he already knew that Thea couldn't be his, still, it re-shattered him, as this truth unveiled.

'*He is handsome*' he had thought after seeing Thea's love, a Knight, '*and thus, a real human. Only if I could be like him, maybe she would love me. Fine, she won't love me, for she is in love with this knight, but she won't at least abhor me the way she does now. Only if I could be like him, then she won't hate me.'* And his eyes had gleamed. *'And yes, I can be like him, Why Can't I? I invent and create so many things… I can recreate myself as well.'* He had danced with joy like a fool, a fool of love of course.

Thus, a new routine had begun. Every day, he would watch the knight from a distance, carefully hiding his own presence. And back at his place, he would practice behaving like him. Soon, he came to realize that both of them had almost the same physical built, which made his work a bit easier of course. The more he followed him, the more he appreciated the knight, for he was helpful and he was kind. *'He is just like me,'* he used to think, *'and yet, we are not at all alike'*.

It was just the face now. *'Why don't I make myself a face?'* he once thought. Thus, a new madness began. Every day, silently, he would follow the knight and watch him. Then, he would practice to be like him by dressing like him, walking like him, talking like him and behaving like him. While this happened, he worked on making a mask; he worked hard and harder to make it perfect by adding imperfections of the Knight's face. He, still, would follow and helplessly watch Thea. *'Someday,'* he would often think, *'she will stop abominating me and that is all I want.'*

She stood there on the river banks for a while as she watched the young knight disappear in the distant horizon. The sound of war-drums was also fading, indicating that the army was on its way to war. Cool breeze blew over the fields, trying to tickle her tears. Dusk had begun.

Every day, she would wait for her knight at the end of the fields. Days passed and the seasons changed, and she kept waiting. But then one night-

One night, she woke up from her sleep when a knock on the door, heard she. She opened the door and was surprised. Stood outside, her beloved knight. So long of waiting she had been through that she doubted if she was seeing the truth. *'Can it be a dream again?'* she thought, *'No, in no dream could she see her knight as perfect as he was now.'* But to make sure she pinched herself and then, with happiness, she embraced her knight, for he was back home. And at that moment, she was the happiest soul.

"You took so long to come back," she smiled and said.

"I know... Thea," He replied.

And at this moment, the maiden realized that something was wrong with her knight. *'Did he call me Thea?'* she thought, *'Never does he do that. I am his Soulmate. His voice, too, is different.'* She stepped back, trying to identify who this person was. His physical appearance was same- his built, his way of standing, walking and talking, even his face looked perfectly the same, but...

A mask is a mask and not a face and the feelings and emotions it does not express. A mask may hide someone's ugliness, but the real person can never be contained.

And she knew that the person was not her knight.

"Who are you?" She asked as she walked towards him and pulled off his mask.

And to her horror, it was the monster she knew. "*You monster, you came again!*" she screamed as she started losing her senses with fright.

He stood there for a while; a drop of tear trickled down his face. He had failed himself and her again. He watched her fainting and falling down, too afraid to go near her again. And he started walking away, away to his hills. '*But haven't I been running away for so long?*' he thought '*Maybe it's time that she sees the real 'me' and not the monster that the world sees. Yes, I will take her to my home. Is it the right thing to do? Why not? I don't intend to harm her, nor do I expect her to love me back. She is meant for the young knight. But I just want her to understand that I am not a monster. And even if a single person knows this, then I can live and die in peace.*' So, he turned back again, towards where the maiden lay on the floor. He lifted her up and silently, started walking towards his home.

She woke up as she felt the warmth of light on her face. She wondered if she was dead as she opened her eyes, 'cause this place definitely did not belong to this world, so beautiful it was. She sat upright, in surprise. From the crystal floor to the marble pillars to the transparent glass ceiling, this place was perfect to be called heaven. She wondered if the piles of books were really touching the roof. "*Who reads so much?*" she started questioning herself, "*Did I hear birds singing? Yes, I did.*" She looked at the birds; none of them were in cages. All were freely flying inside the house, hopping from one branch to the other. "*What?*" she mumbled again as she saw the small forest inside the house. "*What is that beautiful piece of music I hear?*" She followed the sound, the music, to a room on the other side. So many beautiful toys welcomed her, all the clockworks around, and came music from a beautiful piece of clockwork towards which she walked. Then, she saw him- the monster; yes, the monster who brought her here. And she forgot all about the wonders she had seen around. The monster, realizing her presence, quickly put on the mask of the knight in order to hide his ugly face.

He saw her running back to another room. He sighed and grunted, '*Can I not get anything other than despise?*'

As night fell, the wonders became more wondrous. Sky showered stars through the glass roof, which almost turned milky with the light, appearing to be a giant piece of cloud. A million fireflies filled the house with fluorescence and they reflected on the crystal floor, thus creating a panorama of unimaginable beauty. She almost forgot why she was there. The monster silently watched her from a distance, trying to pull together, the broken pieces of his heart.

Days passed. He thought of talking to her, but he still feared his own monstrosity. He would keep his face covered with the mask all the time.

She, on the other hand, was trying to understand the nature of this strange creature. He did not seem so bad to her. He never even harmed her. In fact, she often saw her leaving the place with a sack of toys. Now, she understood the secret of the heavenly toys. '*So was he... But don't they call him a monster? What if all this is but an illusion? If it's not, then why has he kept me captivated? Is he trying to separate me from my love- my beloved knight? Yes, perhaps that's why he dresses and behaves like him as well. He wants to be him. He wants to steal me. No, I should not let that happen. But what if there is some different story to it? What if he actually is a good but a different human and not a monster? But why this place looks to me like some sort of sorcery? Why doesn't he let me go back to my love, my knight?'* She was surrounded with perennial questions, the answers to which were known only to the person or the monster watching her silently, afraid to scare her again.

Few days more, and one night, he decided to speak to her. He smiled as he walked towards her, still dressed as the knight, as had become his habit; he had put on the mask again so that he wouldn't scare the maiden when he told him his story. But then, the maiden surprised her. She saw him and ran towards him, she, then, held him in her arms. Softly, she whispered, "*I am sorry. I think I know your story now.*"

He looked at her with disbelief, thinking of what to say and where to begin, '*She knows my story? No, she does not.'*

"*I do not intend on keeping you a captive here,*" he started with a broken voice, "*I just…*" he waited to pick up the right words from the flood of words and emotions going on inside, so many stories to tell.

She felt his body go loose. This was the moment she was waiting for and time she wasted no more. She pulled the dagger off his waist and hard she impaled it into his chest. "*I know your story, you monster. All you want is to steal me from my beloved knight. I won't let that happen. Did you think that your sorcery, the illusions of this place, your black magic will fool me? No, they won't because they can't.*" She kept stabbing him. She seized the keys from him and ran out of the place, skeptic if the monster had died, for she had heard rumors that he couldn't be killed. Monsters are not supposed to die this way. Fear was all over her now. She ran back towards her home. Her feet bruised and she left a trail of blood as she ran. In her cottage, as she entered, happened what she feared. In the moonlight, she saw a silhouette of the knight who, she was sure, was no one but the monster himself. As he scurried towards her, she leaped on him and slit his throat before he spoke. And she ran out and kept running towards the end of the fields, oblivious that the man, she just killed, tried to say '*Soulmate*' before he drew his last breath. Unnoticed went the thick black thread round his neck that had, perhaps, protected him from all the evil, but love took him down. So many days he had spent waiting for her at the river banks, unaware where she was, scared he had been.

The maiden waited at the end of the fields. She waited for her beloved knight, afraid that the monster would come again, while the monster slept peacefully under the stars. She waited on the river banks till she succumbed to all the love and the sufferings of love. Fools, they all were- fools of love, of course, all doomed by love.

PSEUNAEPIUM

The faint yellow light of the jeep did the least to fight away the dark and mist. Though the driver seemed to be efficient and experienced, assuring Dr. Bose that he was safe, Dr. Bose found his discomfort rising as they neared their destination- Kurseong. '*I have never liked hills,*' he thought to himself, '*I like seas and beaches. They are warm and welcoming, and it's easy to travel to such places. Hills, on the other hand, are cold and they unwelcome you by greeting you with the crooked serpents of roads and landslides.*' Tonight, though, he knew that he had no choice.

Joydeep Sen was a very close friend of Dr. Bose. Together, they had studied, together, they had become doctors, and together, they had worked on most of their research programs. Despite starting careers together as Psychiatrists, Joydeep, in a very short span of time, had gained more fame because of his scientific breakthroughs. But it was all a history now. Twenty-nine years back, when delirium took away his beloved wife, Joydeep went mad. Bereavement, of course, was one reason for his madness, but the major reason was that he could not save his wife from dementia even when this was his area of expertise. This ate him for days, and he would spend his days and nights in his laboratory after this incident. Then, one day, he just disappeared. No one knew where he went; no one, till this morning.

Soon, Dr. Joydeep Sen and his accomplice in scientific crimes, Dr. Parthajit Bose, were forgotten by the world. Even Dr. Bose had started forgetting about the glorious days. So, he certainly was not expecting any telegram this morning as he opened the door to a postman. He read the telegram twice or thrice, just to confirm that his own mind was not playing tricks on his vision. '*Can this be someone's prank?*' he had first thought, but then he read again and he checked the address, '*No, it can't be. Who would remember us? Who would send me a telegram from… from Kurseong?*' He had found it difficult to believe his own eyes. The address was of an old bungalow in Kurseong. He knew the bungalow very well; it was Joydeep's ancestral house.

He had immediately taken a flight from Kolkata to Bagdogra and from there, he had hired a Jeep to Kurseong. Considering his age, which was about to touch sixty one soon, the journey had been a little tough on him. By now, he was starving as well, but the excitement of meeting his old friend gave him a bite of zeal. '*Where did he disappear? Why did he not inform anyone? But most importantly, why did he go and what makes him come back after so long?*' so many questions stormed Dr. Bose's mind and he expected to find all the answers soon. '*Sooner,*' he thought as the jeep screeched to a halt in front of an old bungalow, which, under the dim moonlight, looked like a haunted house from a horror story. Bose admired the British architecture of the house as he got down from the jeep. He had come to this place many times, but mostly during daytimes. Also, he noticed that the surroundings seemed to be lifeless and uninhabited unlike the old times.

"Are you sure that this is the address?" asked the driver, *"No one lives in these houses anymore, but the address you showed me leads to this place, Saab. You can confirm if this is the address. I will wait till you get inside; otherwise I can take you to some hotel."*

Dr. Bose walked up to the door, knocked and waited. Moments later, he heard noises of some crashing and falling from inside, and then, someone opened the door. He could make nothing of the silhouette of this person till he came out in the moonlight. Even then, it was difficult for Dr. Bose to recognize him. Dreaded face, sleep-deprived and tired eyes, bald head, bloodless skin, and grey, shabby beard-Bose, at first, thought that he had come to a wrong address; he was about to apologize and leave, but then the person spoke, *"It has been a while, hasn't it, my old friend?"* He stepped forward and hugged him saying, *"Old friend, you look old."*

"Joy?" Bose asked, still not sure if it was the same person who he came to meet.

"Yes, of course. I know that I am not looking my best today, but this is not why you are here, are you? Of course not, so come inside and warm up yourself with a glass of Brandi, and then, we got a lot to catch up on," Joydeep said, scratching his beard.

Bose, who was not so sure what to say, motioned the jeep driver to leave as he walked inside, following his host.

"If it makes you feel any better, I can apologize for the load-shedding, the reason for this darkness, but I can assure you that I am not the cause of it," Joy spoke and laughed as he carefully guided Dr. Bose across a hallway using a flickering torchlight. Though the moonlight from the window and the torchlight revealed no furniture or anything in this hallway, Bose was feeling trapped in some closed chamber. As far as he recalled, he never had a history of claustrophobia, yet he felt uncomfortable at the moment. What disturbed him more was a putrefying pungent smell that filled the place. A little later, Bose found himself seated in a small room while Joy lit candles and placed them on a small table. As Joy went out to get some food and drink for Bose, Bose realized that the smell had grown stronger; it smelled as if something or someone was dead.

Bose sat with his handkerchief over his nose, trying to block away the smell, hoping that it was not what he thought it to be. Bad thoughts were troubling him now.

"I am sorry about the ambience. I sold all the furniture and everything from this house to fund my experiments. This is the only room where you can make yourself a little comfortable," Joy spoke, walking in, *"and I am sorry about the smell. Just dead lab rats. I will throw them out tomorrow…"*

"Wait. Lab rats? Sold furniture? Will you speak anything that makes sense to me?" Bose asked.

"All in right time, my friend. Why in a hurry? First, make yourself comfortable." Joy offered Bose a glass of drink and a sandwich as he sat on a chair on the other side of the table.

Bose emptied the contents of the glass and uttered, *"Since when did you start having this shit?"*

"Oh! Not shit. It's good Brandi," Joy winked and replied.

"Yeah, sure," Bose distastefully remarked at the taste of the Brandi as he sat back on the worn out couch.

"I am sure that you must be waiting to hurl all those questions at me," Joy said.

"You are a man of psychiatry. Why don't you read them out for me?" Bose was definitely getting restless for answers, but he did not know where to start.

"Not 'You are', the correct usage of words would be 'We are men of Psychiatry'," smilingly said Joy, *"and that is the reason we are here tonight."*

"Why? To make correct use of words?" Dr. Bose mocked him.

"No. Psychiatry, of course," Joy replied and they both chuckled. *"But before I answer your questions, I would like to show you something,"* Joy spoke and walked out of the room.

Dr. Bose sat alone in the room. The effect of smell had mitigated as the effect of Brandi grasped him. He took a bite of the cold sandwich and placed it back on the plate. Actually, he was far from hungry now. All he needed was some answers and the truth.

"Won't it be great if you could easily access other human brains?" Joy said as he walked in with a huge pile of papers and books in his hands.

"What? Accessing human brains? We do try studying the human brain using EEG or Electroencephalography and sometimes hypnosis. Don't we? Is this what you mean by accessing brain? That's a fancy term by the way. I like it," Bose said, amused.

Joy seemed to be a bit agitated at the response but he calmly spoke, "*In EEG, we record the electrical activity of the brain and test brain's functioning, and in hypnosis, it is the subject who explores his mind, we just act as agents who provoke them to look inside.*" He placed the books and papers on the table as he continued, "*There are times when merely looking into a recorded analysis on a piece of paper does not work and there are situations when the subject is incapable of exploring his own mind.*"

"*Yes, there are such cases and there are a lot of therapies and then, there is electroconvulsive...*" Bose started but was interrupted.

"*Therapies? Being a Psychiatrist, even you know that therapies don't always give permanent solutions. No therapy can guarantee a hundred percent cure, and there are diseases which even therapies and medicines can't cure... like... like Alzheimer's disease.*"

"*So... What do you suggest?*"

"*What I am saying is that if experts like us could directly connect to the subject's brain, that is, we look inside his mind and explore out the problems by feeling them through our brain... then... then, not only can we understand the subject's real crisis, but we also can provide him with a permanent cure.*"

"*Interesting thought, but how do you think we can do that?*" Bose humored him.

"*Well, answer the most basic question- how does a human brain work?*"

"*Electric signals... Neurons carry signals to and from the brain. Each and every part of the body, when senses something, the neurons carry electrical signals to the brain and then the brain sends the required stimulus to that part in the form of signals again. Sometimes, in fact... Wait a minute... why are you asking me this basic stuff?"* Bose seemed to be a bit perplexed.

Joy laughed a little and then spoke, *"And thoughts? You agree that thoughts are also a type of electric signal?"*

"Yes, I believe so."

"So, you agree that the human brain is continuously emitting electric signals at a certain frequency so low and feeble that man-made antennas and transponders can't detect these signals?"

"Yes, I believe so. There are many theories which..."

"And you agree that brains also act as receivers?"

"Maybe... Maybe yes, brain picks up on electrical signals even when it is not directly applied, thus the most debatable concept of sixth sense." Bose bluntly replied, though a bit intrigued.

"So let me summarize- A brain stores everything in the form of electric signals and it is continuously interacting with the world by emitting and receiving electric signals."

"Yes... yes for the nth time."

"So, all we need is an antenna, a transponder to connect to and communicate with a human brain, and our own brains are capable of answering to this situation"

"That is?"

"Our brain, as you know, works at a very low average efficiency- ten percent on an average. But if we boost up this efficiency, then human brain can emit these thoughts or signals in a receivable and understandable form. I mean to say, all we need is another brain, of course, with boosted efficiency, to receive and interpret these signals and to further communicate."

"I don't understand."

Devashish Acharya

"*In simple words, if we increase both, my and my subject's brain's efficiency, and if we establish a proper communication channel between our brains, then our brains can communicate effectively with each other, that is, I can connect to the subject's brain directly. In case I just want this communication to be one way, all I will have to do is keep my brain's efficiency a bit higher so that his brain does not interfere with my signals or thoughts and thus my brain. Then, I can look into his mind as if it is all happening inside me. This will, of course, need a proper synchronization and a common channel along with a lot of practice in the form of meditation. Once this connection is established, I can not only read his mind, but I can also modify the signals and thus... the subject's thoughts.*" Joy sat up straight with a glow of happiness on his face.

"*Wait... wait... wait... Now what do you suggest this communication channel should be?*"

"*Well, I thought that you will have it figured out yourself. Anyways, we, first, need to bring both the minds on a common ground. This can happen only when they both are thinking or feeling the same thing. Then only, they can communicate with each other. Of course, our brains are sensing, thinking and feeling a lot of things simultaneously, but a common thing, which has to be strong enough for both the brains to sense, can help provide a kind of synchronization, thus connecting the minds. Whatever... the five forms of senses- touch, smell, vision, taste and listening can be used as channels. Of these, using touch and taste as common channels is not always possible. But the remaining three can bring our brains to a common channel, thus making the connection possible.*"

Bose kept staring blankly with disbelief and then spoke, *"And you say that subject's thoughts can be modified as well, how?"*

"It is simple. All you need to do is interfering with the original signal and altering or modifying them accordingly. For example, you know that our eyes only capture the light; it's the brain that interprets and generates images or visions, right?

"Yes."

"So, if you interfere those vision-generating signals and modify them according to your wish, you can actually plant a different vision altogether in the subject's brain. Then, he won't be seeing what his eyes are seeing, but he will be seeing what you want to show him. It's the same with all other senses." Joy sat back with a sense of pride on his face.

"And the subject doesn't even realize that he is being fooled?"

"It is not fooling them." Joy almost lost his temper. *"Just think about the zillion ways this technology can help the various patients suffering from Schizophrenia, Parkinson's disease, Wernicke-Korsakoff Syndrome, Alzheimer's disease and many other forms of Dementia and Paranoia. All we need to do is planting an alternate reality in the subject's mind. Not only will it provide us with unimaginable insights of the human mind, you never know what other wonders and answers may get revealed. And if properly practiced, a single person can read and manipulate several human minds at once."*

"And how will this all happen?" Bose keenly asked.

"Pseunaepium is the answer."

"What opium?"

"Not opium, it's Pseunaepium; that's what I call it- a serum that can boost up human brain's efficiency."

"You think it is pos-"

"*Possible? Yes, it is. Just look at these.*" Joy motioned towards the pile of papers he had brought in. "*I have read ancient science, medicine, mythology, cult and others to understand the concept of comprehending human brains. All through human history, they have spoken about people possessing the power of reading human minds. May it be telepathy, time travel, astral projections or superficial visions; various methods, all religions, customs and countries have spoken about it in different forms, and I have done a lot of study. This all cannot be just some myth. And I believe that... that such a serum is possible. It's controlling the human brain that is the most difficult part; that may require a lot of practice.*" Joy spoke it all in just one breath apparently.

"*It sounds really good Joy... but...*"

"*But still, you don't believe that it is possible, right?*"

"*No... it's not like...*"

"*Don't call yourself a man of science.*" Joy stood up, fuming. "*Skepticism is a good thing; it makes us work towards finding the truth; believing without reason is damaging, but disbelieving without any proof is catastrophic. That's not what science teaches us. Before Newton explained it, gravity was considered to be a supernatural act, and before the Wright brothers invented, airplanes were considered to be fairy tales. But they worked towards finding the truth unlike you... You won't even want to know the truth... but just believe that it is not possible.*"

"*I am not saying that I completely disbelieve, but the powers of this single serum, as you explained, stretches the limits of plausibility too far,*" Bose replied, surprised at Joy's temper.

"*I need your help, Bose,*" Joy pleaded, "*We can create this miracle for mankind.*"

"*I don't know, Joy. Why don't you come to Kolkata with me? We can think about it later.*" Dr. Bose was getting restless now.

"*So you don't believe me. And I don't think that there is a way that I can make you believe like this. So... follow me. There is only one thing I can do.*"

"*What? Where?*"

"*Just follow. I need to show you something else- something that may change your mind.*" Joy stood up and started walking out of the room while Bose followed.

They walked through a long corridor, guided by torchlight, till Joy stopped by a door and opened it up. The door opened to a staircase which descended to a basement. Joy motioned Bose to follow, but Bose didn't seem to have a nice feeling about this. As they reached the basement, Bose screamed with horror as the torchlight revealed three people tied and barbed on chairs. Even in this dim light, he recognized the faces of these three people- Dr. Venkat, Dr. Nath and Dr. Shikha- all ex-colleagues.

"*I asked them to help me, but they denied. I have a lot of expectations from you, Bose. Together, we can achieve what they call 'impossible'. The final decision remains with you though,*" Joy whispered and grinned.

Bose turned back to look at Joy. He felt that he didn't even know this person. There was something so cruel in his gaze that he felt losing his own senses. He felt weak inside; he needed to hold on to something for support. Then, he heard a loud laughter.

With that laughter, he saw that everything around was quickly disappearing. He looked back and the corpses were gone. He looked back again at Joy who seemed to be disappearing into thin air, the staircase, the basement, everything- it all disappeared in no time and Bose, again, found himself sitting in the same small cabin, alone. His heart beat had increased as if racing against the flickering candlelight. He wanted to run away, but he could not feel his feet at that moment. Then, he again heard a loud burst of laughter and the door opened. Bose tightly clung onto the arm of the chair as he saw Joydeep walking in.

"How was my little show of imagination?" Joy asked as he walked in, smiling with an expression of accomplishment all over his face.

"Ima... wh... no... imagination?" Bose took a minute or two to feel back his tongue.

"Yes." Joy took out a small glass bottle from his pocket. *"I present to you Pseunaepium."*

"So, this was all..."

"I apologize for all this, but I wanted you to believe me, and so, I thought of giving you a glimpse of what this amazing serum can do. I had put a few drops of this in your Brandi, while I myself took a higher dose in order to manipulate your brain without you knowing about it. I got a local guy to arrange dead mice for this purpose so... so that we could connect through common smell, as I explained, to bring our brains on a common ground, and the strong pungent smell did well." Joy smiled *"Do you remember me going out to bring a pile of papers?"*

"Yes," Bose replied, frantically.

"I never came back actually."

Bose now noticed the pile of papers missing from the table. *"So... this game of imagination began then and there itself?"*

"*I was able to connect with you as soon as you finished your drink because I have been practicing this technique on local people for the past six years. You see, I am the reason most of the neighbors have evacuated their houses. They thought that I was mad.*" He paused, chuckled and continued, "*While you were sitting here, I went to the other room and started showing you an illusion. Though the last part of the illusion was not planned, I thought that it's better to have a little drama. Moreover, I looked inside you and knew that you won't suffer any panic attack. You, my friend, never spoke a word or left this couch. In reality, all this while, you sat alone and you actually relished that cold sandwich.*" Joy pointed at the empty plate. "*All this was actually happening inside your brain. Yes, I had to control all your senses, which I think I did successfully. Had I not told you about it, you would have lived and died with this as a reality. I read your thoughts as well, along with your secrets. Sorry for that intrusion. Don't worry; all your dirty little secrets are safe with me… But you actually thought that I am a psycho killer.*"

Bose smiled sheepishly and feebly, still not out of shock. "*So you did it. Why do you need my help then?*"

Joy smiled and held up the bottle of Pseunaepium high "*Look at this. This is the little amount I am left with; and for our purpose, we will need a lot of it. We will study the contents of this bottle and together, we will develop more of this so that the world can elicit benefits from it. I can't do this alone. It took me more than twenty years to develop this. In fact, a major component of this serum comes from the Himalayas. I had gone there in search of answers, and I met a hermit who could not only read human minds but could also understand what animals were thinking. After I requested a lot, he gave me a small bottle with a green liquid in it. He told me that it helped him in reading minds. He, though, did not tell me what this liquid was. I even tried to study the liquid, but it was complex. It kept changing its molecular structure. I used that liquid to prepare the serum. Even the final serum is very volatile in nature. I had documented the formulae of all the various chemicals this serum uses, but a month back, I lost those documents in a fire. I lost everything. I went back to the Himalayas in search of that Hermit, but I couldn't find him. Now, we need to study the serum properly in order to recreate it, and I can't do this on my own again; but we, together, will redefine everything.*" Joy held up the bottle high and proudly looked at it.

Bose looked at Joy more proudly. *'He is going to make a comeback with another breathtaking breakthrough,'* he thought and he stood up to greet and congratulate his old friend with a hug. But the shock, perhaps, had still not left his body completely as he lost his balance while he walked towards Joy, stumbled on the table and almost fell over Joy who lost his balance. Fell off from his hand, the bottle that contained the miracle- **Pseunaepium**. In the silence, they heard the breaking of a glass bottle. In the flickering candle-light, stared blankly at each other, two pairs of horrified eyes while silence did the talking for them.

HAUNTING WITH HUMOR

It was an early autumn dusk, and the cool autumn breeze was teasing the fallen leaves. The shy pond playfully looked up at the sky, and the sky sent a gush of wind to caress its own self in the pond's glassy eyes. Someone, in the vicinity, blew a shell conch and many others followed. Welcoming the Goddess of fortune every evening by offering prayers and blowing conch is a ritual in almost every Bengali household. A swarm of *Babus* and Clerks merrily walked back to their homes as the kids sadly said goodbye to their playground and the last flock of birds flew back to their nests.

Joga felt that he was the busiest person on earth at the moment as he looked at the crowd waiting for tea and snacks. *"Joga's Tea Stole"* read the sign board fixed atop his tea stall. Joga was really busy preparing tea and serving samosas. He had, many times, thought of hiring a helping hand, but the thought always gave him shivers as it reminded him of the last time when he had hired a kid to help him serve tea. *Thana's Bada Babu* had threatened to imprison him for indulging in child labor when he saw that kid. Joga had immediately dismissed the kid. He didn't even dare to ask the kid to return the three months' advance he had paid him. Even today, he did not know what his crime was and what child labor meant. According to him, he was only helping a mishap child.

"Policemen are not easy to understand," Fotik, a *rickshaw-wala,* had told him, *"but you should never disobey them. They can do whatever they want to."*

Joga believed him. In fact, he had always believed that *riskshaw-walas* were very clever and wise as they interacted with all kinds of people every day. Whatever his crime was, never again did Joga consider hiring a new guy. Moreover, he was worried about his reputation he had established amongst the people of *Shantigram*. After all, people loved him very much. In fact, four years back some kids even gave him a fancy nickname- 'Jogs'. Everyone started calling him by that name. But with time, his name got modified even further. Some other kids, who interpreted the name in a different way, started calling him 'Jokes' and now everyone, starting from the seventy something *Khuro* (uncle) to the fifteen years old *Piklu* called him 'Jokes'. Now, he was *Jokes Da'* for everyone in the village.

Few days back, Bapi, the self-proclaimed hero of the *Para*, had even told him that he had created a page on Facebook- *"Jokes' Adda"*. Joga did not know what Facebook was. He had simply assumed that it was some kind of an address book or a teenage magazine. He could not suppress his joy over the thought of his small tea-stall being mentioned in a magazine. That day, Bapi and his friends were treated with free tea and free *samosas*. Although, later, he had wondered why the book-store owner, Dayal *Kaka*, had laughed when Joga had told him that he wanted to buy a Facebook.

"Jealousy," he had thought, *"The old man must be jealous of my success. After all, the major reason these people have failed to succeed is their inability to see others succeed. Instead of working hard to get success, these people work harder to pull others down. In any case, what would I do with the magazine? I won't be able to read it. Maybe, when I meet Bapi next, I will ask him what they wrote about me."* But it had been a few days that Bapi had not paid him a visit. Rumors were that he had run away with a girl from Monipukur *Para*- the arch-rivals of Shantigram.

———◆◆◆———

Everyone was busy in Shantigram, but when asked, no one could roll out a reason for why they were busy. Shantigram had always been like this. Nothing 'happening' ever happened in this small town. The last time the town had seen some activity was when Shantigram football club won IPL (Indrapur Premiere League). Although, the place had seen glorious days when it was a part of a small kingdom, but apart from an old temple and the ruins of *Rajbari*, the palace, nothing remained of the town's glorious past. The temple was still in use and several people came from other towns and villages to offer their prayers to *Goddess Kali* every day. Rajbari, though, remained in ruins. But recently, a group of people had come to the town. They would work restlessly around the temple with their machines. When asked, they would say that they were government officials working to restore the temple and the palace. This had given a new hope to the people of Shantigram. They had started imagining how much better their lives would become once the place became a tourist spot. Many had, in fact, started planning their business accordingly.

———◆◆◆———

Joga peeped out of his stall. "Nah! It definitely is going to rain tonight. I should close my stall early," he said to Gagan *Babu* who seemed to be lost in the newspaper. Joga, then, looked at the group of teenagers who had just arrived. Sometimes, Joga, while listening to them, would wonder if the most important decisions in the world were made in his stall; such was the zeal in these guys while discussing politics, football, cricket, movies and songs. On many occasions, one of them would lose temper and there would be a brawl of words. But that didn't concern him. He was sure about one thing that Bengalis won't use hands to fight though they would kill each other with words. Today's heated discussion was about ghosts. Upon hearing the conversation, Joga started reciting *Ram-Naam*.

He left the stall at around 8:00 pm. While heading towards his house, he looked at the flickering lamps of the ancient *Kali-Temple*. He could hear the bells of the temple and the hymns being sung by the *pundits*. It meant that the evening *aarti* was still on. He stopped, turned towards the temple, folded his hands and said his prayers. His house was just a few yards away from the temple, but the irony was that he had never been to the temple; he was not allowed to.

Joga's great grandfather used to be the head priest of this temple. The local legend said that the Goddess herself appeared in the king's dream and ordered him to construct a temple for the prosperity of his kingdom. The King obeyed and constructed this stupendous temple. Also, a three foot tall statue of the Goddess, entirely made of gold and studded with precious gems, was placed in the temple. Joga's great grandfather was made the head priest and was given the responsibility to take care of the temple. He worked hard for several years. But one night, he disappeared along with the golden statue of the Goddess. People believed that he stole the statue and evaded with it, leaving behind his family. His family was banished from the kingdom for generations.

Though Joga returned back to the place after generations, he was still not allowed to enter the temple premises. This made Joga upset sometimes. He had lost his parents at a very young age, he had never gone to school like other kids and he was not even allowed to set foot in the temple. He often wondered how many more generations of his family would have to atone and suffer because of his great grandfather's sin.

There were other legends about the temple as well. There were local folklores about the *tantriks* who used to perform magic in the temple. Some even believed that there was a magical temple inside the temple. But these all were a part of the local fairytales.

Joga had an ancestral house built by his forefathers in this town, but it was in ruins, making it impossible for anyone to live in it. He, sometimes, thought of repairing that house, but he did not have the money for that. His preceding generations had been stripped off of wealth and glory. Only an old gold amulet remained as his family fortune, which he inherited from his mother. It bore his family symbol- the sun and the moon together in one body.

Joga unlocked the door with a heavy heart. He had a single room to call a house that he had rented from Binoy *Khuro*. In fact, it was Binoy *Khuro* who helped Joga come back to the town and set up a tea stall. But this house stood aloof from the others in the vicinity. Not everyone had fully accepted him in the society yet. Some still believed that he was cursed for the sins of his forefather.

Under the dim light of a single bulb, he stirred the pot of rice while steam filled the room. He was thinking about the temple and his great grandfather, but his thoughts were interrupted by some noise in the room.

"*Mimi,*" Joga called out the name of his pet cat. "*Is that you? Stop chasing rats now.*"

The noise stopped within moments. He was not sure if he actually heard someone whispering into his ears, "*You idiot! This exactly is what I expect from you; talking to a stupid cat... Huh!*"

He turned around and saw no one. He was not surprised. This had happened to him before as well. On many occasions, he had heard someone whispering words like fool, moron, idiot and stupid when he was alone in the room. He had informed Fotik about it, who had told him that it was the voice of his *Antaratma,* his inner conscience.

"*Fotik knows so much,*" he spoke to himself in a low voice, "*That is why I always give him tea for free.*"

"*Yeah, you couldn't be any dumber,*" the voice whispered again.

Bapi had once recorded Joga's voice on his cellphone and Joga had heard the recording. This voice and the voice he had heard in the recording were exactly the same, confirming his belief that it was him speaking to himself.

"Nah! It's time to have dinner and go to sleep. My Antaratma is getting restless tonight," he thought.

Mimi was nowhere to be seen, so he had his dinner alone and went to sleep. Just as he closed his eyes, he heard the voice again, *"Bah! Good for nothing."*

"I have heard so many stories about people getting motivated by their inner conscience; I wonder why mine humiliates me," Joga mumbled with agitation and closed his eyes again.

Wondering about Bapi and what was published in the Facebook magazine, he didn't realize when sleep possessed him, but he was woken up by a sudden noise in the room. Startled, he sat up and started searching his torch, hoping that it was Mimi, but he heard the voice again.

"Not on your left, the torch is on your right," the voice spoke in the darkness of the room.

Joga's hands located the torch and he was about to switch it on when the voice spoke again, *"Torch won't make any difference."*

Joga lit the torch and looked around. Door and windows were closed. No one was around.

"Wh… ho… who… who…" he tried to ask in a quivering tone.

"Ah! Stop hooting like an owl now." The voice sounded irritated.

"Please tell me who you are," Joga asked in a very meek voice *"Are you my Antaratma?"*

"Am I? Since when did your 'Antaratma' become as intelligent as I am?" the voice asked in a mocking tone.

In a shaky voice, Joga spoke again, throwing torchlight in all the possible directions, *"You are my Antaratma, and you should motivate me, not mock me."*

"Huh! Motivate you? For what? To prepare tea and samosas?" The voice snorted.

"Hey! What is your problem? Will you stop being rude?" Joga gritted his teeth.

"Yes, if you stop being so stupid," replied the voice.

"If I am stupid then so are you because you are a part of me," Joga firmly said.

"Stop offending me by calling me your Antaratma. I am, by no means, a part of you," the voice said, angrily.

"Then who are you?" enquired Joga, scared a little, as he thought about all the possible answers to this question, *"And why can't I see you?"*

"That's the whole point," the voice spoke with a sigh, *"You cannot see me. It took me continuous practice for almost a century to be able to make myself audible to humans. Sometimes, I can also make myself partly visible, but I don't know how much more will it take to be completely visible."* The voice sounded a bit upset.

Joga let the torch fall from his hand. The torch crashed with a loud noise on the floor and then there was a deafening silence and dark.

"Ittt...It means th-th-that y-you are a..." Joga tried to speak but his tongue betrayed.

"Ghost? Yes, you may call me that," the voice said with a soft sound of a chuckle.

But Joga did not wait for the voice to speak any more. He was already running around the room, trying to locate the door as he started chanting *Hanuman Chalisa* at the pitch of his voice, *"Jai Hanuman Guna-Gyaana-Saagar, Jai Kapish…"* But he was interrupted again as the voice laughed and said, *"Wrong chant. Its 'Gyaan-Guna-Sagar' and not 'Guna-Gyaana-sagar',"* the voice continued with a loud laughter, *"Such pity! You even seem to offend the Gods."*

"Aren't you a ghost?" Joga asked in a trembling voice.

"So? Are all ghosts same or what? Who told you that every ghost is afraid of chants of the Gods?"

By this time, Joga had located the door and he was about to unlatch it when he felt a hand on his shoulder, and the voice spoke again, *"Don't go out through the door. It is dangerous."*

"Why of course! Staying locked with a ghost in the dark makes me feel very safe," Joga blurted with fear.

Then he felt someone pulling him back, and the voice yelled at him, *"If you ever knew the number of times and the number of ways I have saved you, you would be more than thankful to me."*

"Saved me? What for? So that you could kill me by giving me a heart attack tonight?" Joga asked, stammering.

"Heart attack? No… Beheading you would be more of my style," the voice echoed, followed by laughter.

"Be… Beheading?" Joga almost imagined himself getting decapitated. The sight was not very pleasant.

"Yes, but not tonight. Tonight, you got a lot to do. In the next ten minutes, you have to go to the temple," the voice softly spoke.

"A lot to do? Go to the temple? What are you saying? You only said that I should not go out as it is dangerous," Joga spoke, wondering if he was amidst one of his many meaningless dreams, for the current situation was not making any sense to him.

"Shut up, will you?" the voice shouted, *"It was not safe then, but it will be safe within the next ten minutes."*

Joga wanted to ask what was going on, but he decided to keep quiet for the sake of his head. He stood in the dark, amidst the deafening silence for a few minutes. He was not able to understand how much time went by. So, he finally broke his silence, *"Where are you, dear ghost?"*

There was no reply for a while. Joga felt more scared. He could not understand why the idea of being with a ghost seemed to be more comfortable than being left alone in the dark now.

"I am going to scream out of fear now," Joga said, almost crying out of fear.

"Dhurr Boka*! You always have to blabber. I was having some serious discussion with the others here,"* the voice echoed as if it were standing right next to Joga.

"Others?" the thought of more ghosts in the room gave Joga shivers.

"Yes, others; ghosts of all the prominent people of this place from all the different generations are in this room right now. Everyone has a lot of expectations from you. Now listen carefully. I can't go to the temple with you. The place still haunts me," the voice spoke with a sigh.

"If the place haunts even a ghost, then how do you think that I qualify to go?" Joga touched his neck and throat to make sure that there was no sword pointed at him.

"*Because you won't become a hero sitting over here,*" the voice spoke with a chuckle, "*Don't be afraid. Even the kings are with you tonight. Take your **lathi** (stick) along with you and hold on to it till things are safe. No one can do you any harm. I promise.*" There was so much affection in the voice that it reminded Joga of his own father. The voice continued, "*There are bad people at the temple and…*"

Joga interrupted and said, "*No, you are mistaken. There are some government officials working on the temple's renovation.*"

"*They are the bad people, you moron,*" the voice scolded him, "*and let me complete. They are not government officials. They are here to steal the famous gold statue of **Devi Kali**. You have to stop them. Right now, there are only a few of them working at the temple and they are very close to discovering the statue. But more are coming. You have to reach the statue before they do.*"

Joga waited for a while to make sure that the ghost had done speaking, and then, he politely said, "*Sir, that gold statue was stolen…*"

He could not complete as he heard a soft laughter which was followed by few murmurs and then by the voice, "*You will know soon. Now go.*"

The door creaked open itself. Joga felt that someone handed him his *lathi* and torch. He, then, walked towards the temple with faltering steps.

When he reached the temple, he saw some three or four men lying unconscious at the temple gate. Then he heard an unfamiliar voice, "*It took us almost an hour to haunt them out of their senses.*"

Joga looked around, but saw no one. He was not afraid this time, though he wondered who this new ghost was. It was the first time Joga was entering the temple premise. He closed his eyes, prayed to the Goddess and walked in, feeling glad and proud.

"Behind the temple," the new voice continued, *"they have dug a tunnel. We have to get in through that tunnel to reach the **Patal-Mandir**."*

The word *Patal-Mandir* made sense to Joga. He had always heard people saying that there was a temple inside the temple. He quietly followed the order and went behind the temple. There was actually a tunnel with boring machines and shovels scattered around. He felt a little assured that he was not being guided wrongly. He waited for further instructions, but none came. So he switched on his torch and entered the tunnel. Only silence echoed while his the torchlight guided him through the tunnel. At first, the tunnel seemed to be narrow, but as he went further, he found that the tunnel had broadened. In fact, he observed that now he was seeing carved walls on both the sides as if the tunnel had always existed. There were beautiful carvings on the walls that told the stories of Gods and Goddesses.

After walking for almost fifteen minutes, Joga saw light at the end of the tunnel. He stumbled upon a piece of rock and the noise echoed in the tunnel.

"Shhhh…" the new ghost warned him, *"Keep quiet and switch off your torch. Take them by surprise."*

Joga switched off his torch and quietly stepped towards the end of the tunnel. As he reached the end of the tunnel, he heard some human voices. Instead of being glad, he rather waited for a ghost's voice to guide him. He hid himself behind a giant pillar and carefully looked at the surroundings. It was a humongous circular chamber. There was a large *Shiva Linga* at the center, covered with mosses and shrubs. On the other side of the temple, he saw some ten men trying to break open a huge door. They had fixed lights and torches in the chamber and were carrying some machines. He tried to comprehend the complexity of this situation, but before he could, he found himself running swiftly towards the gang of men. He wondered how he was running when he had not even put an effort to lift his feet, but before he could think more, he had already knocked one of the men out of his senses. And with that, chaos began. One guy tried to attack Joga from the back, but Joga's *lathi* was already on the guy's face. Another tried to stab him with a knife, but Joga jumped high in the air and kicked him to the ground. One guy took out a pistol and started firing, but Joga effortlessly dodged all the bullets. Within moments, he had already disarmed the guy. One after another, within a matter of minutes, all the ten guys lay on the ground. Joga stopped to look at them. He did not, at all, feel exhausted from the fight. He was about to throw away his *lathi* when he heard footsteps. He held his *lathi* firmly and waited for the goons. He saw around fifteen men entering the chamber. They all had *lathis* and guns in their hands. They first looked at their fellow men who were lying on the ground and then at Joga with disbelief. They all charged towards him at once, but before they could shoot at him or reach him, there was a loud noise of gunfire. They all stopped and turned back to look at the source of this gunfire. Joga was also startled. He looked towards the entrance and saw *Thana's Bada Babu* standing there with his force. The goons were taken aback by the presence of Police and tried to run berserk. Some tried to fire at the policemen, but Joga was already charging at them with his *lathi*. Soon, most of the goons were either on the floor, or were begging for their lives. All the policemen, including *Bada Babu*, looked at Joga with wide eyes. Joga looked at the surrendering goons and gladly threw away his *lathi*. He was about to walk towards *Bada Babu* when one of the goons, who was lying on the floor, picked up the *lathi* and hit Joga hard on his head. And then, it was all black. Joga felt like he was falling deeper into an abyss of oblivion.

In a dreamlike vision, Joga saw that he was lying in a large chamber which seemed like a royal chamber. He wondered if his vision was blurred or if he was actually seeing only silhouettes of the people staring at him. He tried to sit up, but could not. His head hurt. Then he heard a very familiar voice, like the voice of his own, the voice he had thought as his *Antaratma, "You moron! You cannot even follow a simple order. Didn't I tell you to hold on to your lathi till everything was over?"*

Joga, instead of answering the question, asked, *"Am I dead?"*

"Ah!" the apparition exclaimed, *"Not yet."*

Joga tried to identify the silhouette he was looking at. It looked like a shadow of his own, as if his own shadow had been separated from him.

"Who are you?" Joga finally asked the right question.

The silhouette leaned towards him and softly spoke, *"I am your great grandfather, Jogeshwar Bhattcharjee. The one because of whom you all had to suffer."*

Joga stared at him the silhouette and asked, *"Did you…"*

"*No, he didn't,*" another voice interrupted. Joga recognized this other voice. It was the same voice that had guided him in the tunnel. He tried to look at the silhouette of this other person. He could not identify it.

"*I am the king,*" this other silhouette continued, "*who built the Kali-Temple and appointed your great grandfather as the head priest,*" he let out a sigh and continued again, "*Once, I was visited by a tantrik. He told me about his great powers and I believed him. In fact, it was his idea to build the Patal-Mandir. I built the Patal-Mandir, which could be reached either by a secret passage of the Kali-Temple, or the Royal* **Devisthaan***. The tantrik would advise me on various religious matters and he started living in the Patal-Mandir. One day, he told me that he had foreseen a plague befalling my kingdom. It made me worried. He also gave me a solution to stop the plague- bringing the golden statue of the Goddess to Patal-Mandir and a human sacrifice. Though I agreed with the first part of the solution, I was against the idea as a whole, but he convinced me that without human sacrifice, the doom was inevitable. Moreover, he told me that only a religious person with a pure heart could be sacrificed for the ritual. So, he picked your great grandfather as a choice for the sacrifice. I didn't want to do it, but I could not imagine the horrors of a plague upon my subjects. So one night, I called Jogeshwar for a late night Puja ceremony. It was there that the Tantrik beheaded him for human sacrifice. His corpse was then buried near the sacrificial alter, as was the ritual. The statue of Goddess was also shifted to the Patal-Mandir that night.*" The voice stopped at this sad note, sighed and continued, "*It was only later that I realized that it was only a trick by the*

Tantrik to get rid of Jogeshwar. He envied Jogeshwar because I always respected him more."

"Then why did you banish us from the kingdom?" Joga asked with a rising anger.

"I did not. The people did. I kept silent to avoid any sort of controversy and loss of faith. I even closed the Patal-Mandir shortly after the incident; and closed, it has remained till these goons came to the town." The King leaned, apparently sat besides Joga and said, *"I apologize for my sin. I still repent for my deeds."*

"And he has repented a lot, son," Jogeshwar spoke, *"In fact, we could have let the goons take away that statue, but it was the King's idea to make you a hero and restore our family name."* Joga felt the warmth of a cold hand on his forehead.

"Now, listen," the king spoke, *"Go to the ruins of the Rajbari tomorrow. Take a shovel with you. From the northern corner of the palace, start walking towards the north-east direction till you reach the ruins of the Devisthaan. From the Devisthaan, start walking east. Stop exactly after 20 yards. Start digging at that spot and continue till you hit an iron door. The door opens to a treasure beyond imagination. But be careful. The spirits of tantriks roam around in that place. Even we are afraid to go to that place. So, you will have to take this adventure alone on your own."*

"Now go back to sleep so that you can wake up, son," his great grandfather gently kissed him on his head.

———◆◆◆———

Joga opened his eyes again. This time, he was lying on a cot. A very familiar human face was staring at him now- Binoy *Khuro*. Joga realized that he was in *Khuro's* house. With some effort and a little help from *Khuro*, Joga sat up.

Thana's Bada Babu was also in the room with many others from the town. He was telling them about the last night's incident, "I was sleeping in my house, unaware of what was happening in the temple, but I woke up with a knock on my window. I was wondering who dared to do such a thing, but then I heard the knock again. It was dark outside and I saw a man standing in the dark, knocking on my window glass. The silhouette looked to me like Joga. I quickly opened the window and only when I heard the man speaking, my doubt was confirmed that it was actually Joga. He quickly told me about the criminals in the temple and then, ran away without waiting for my instructions. It took me some time to gather my men and by the time we reached, Joga had already taken the criminals down. You all should have seen him fighting. It was like an action movie scene."

Joga, at once, knew that it was his great grandfather who informed *Bada Babu*. *Bada Babu* turned towards Joga, got up and walked towards him. He took out a piece of jewel wrapped in plastic from his pocket and handed it to Joga saying, *"See if you can recognize this?"*

It was a golden ring. Joga looked at the symbol on the ring- the sun and the moon together in one body- his family symbol.

"A team of actual government officers arrived this morning to inspect the place after the news of last night's incident reached them. They discovered the golden statue of the Goddess. While excavating, they also unearthed many skeletons and skulls near the statue. On one of these skeletons, they found this ring. We

think… We believe that your great grandfather never stole the statue. I apologize to you on behalf of everyone in the town."

The bookstore owner, Dayal *Kaka,* who had mocked him once, walked towards Joga and unfolded the newspaper in his hand. Joga could not read what was written on it, but he did see his own photograph on the first page of the newspaper.

"*These criminals were actually informed by one of our own pundits that there is a hidden temple according to the legend. The pundit has gone missing, otherwise I would have…*" *Bada Babu* was continuing, but Joga was not paying heed. His eyes were now on a shovel kept in a corner of the room. "*Tomorrow,*" he mumbled, "*another adventure will begin.*"

Only a dream apart

"*It all started with rain and thunder; it seemed as if the Gods of anger above the clouds were growing weary of the peace below. I looked down at my camera while raindrops dripped down through its lens. I saw the rain chasing blood to drains. Then, I lifted up my head and I saw her. Her white wedding gown had gone red with blood. She sat there on the stairs of a chapel, amidst all the doom. She cried and she moaned as she lifted up the head of her dead groom. I tried to look at the groom's face, but the rain blurred my vision while blood defaced his face. The sky seemed to be reflecting earth, as it too went blood-red. I tried to understand what had happened, I tried to comprehend. And with shaky steps, I footed towards her. She sensed it perhaps. She raised her head and she wailed. Her eyes had gone completely red with blood and with rage. The sweet melody of wedding bells, which I could hear until then, was replaced by a deathful dirge. She looked at me, I think, and she screamed and wailed again. I think she was about to say something to me, but then appeared a lady from somewhere behind her- a lady in black. It seemed that she was already dressed for a funeral, not a wedding. The lady in black looked at me and she smiled, then she looked at the bride and smiled again. She stopped the bride from speaking and she whispered something in her ears. I tried to step forward to listen, but then there was a lightning-strike on the roof of the chapel. Black smoke rose with a flash of fire and the black started consuming it all… precipitously. Again, I heard a thunder, a louder one and I woke up… I woke up from the dreadful dream. It's 3:20 am, 12ᵗʰ December, 2013. I have come to the hills to spend some time away from my mundane life on my therapist Dr. Henna's suggestion, but I don't think that it is making things any better,"* Dhruv groaned and sighed as he shifted the recorder to his other hand, then he continued, *"It has been over a year that I am seeing the same dream every damn night. Like always, I couldn't see the groom's face, or hear the voice of that lady in black. Everything else was exactly the same… the beginning, how it ends… every damn thing. Nothing new revealed. My head keeps throbbing and it hurts badly. I will again need one of those pills. Done for tonight, I believe. It's driving me insane."*

Dhruv placed the voice recorder back on the side of the pillow, where he could locate it again if needed. Then he sat up on the bed as he felt his pillow drenched in sweat. He reached for the table lamp on the bedside table and switched it on. With both hands, he tried to rub the dream and sweat off his face. He kept breathing heavily as he looked back at the recorder. His therapist had strictly warned him to record or note down whatever he saw in dreams, whenever he saw, which was almost every night.

"You never know, maybe you will find the solution of your dreams through this dream itself. Maybe, it will reveal to you all the answers someday," Dr. Henna, his therapist, had told him, *"So I strictly advise that you keep a record of your every night's dream."*

He sat there silently after gulping a pill with three glasses of water and he waited for sleep to possess him again. Though, he was afraid of going back to the dream that had haunted him since a forgotten forever.

Dhruv was a wedding photographer by profession. Successful? That he was, but he was still fighting his way to fame. But everything had gone haywire since the past one year. It all started with the dreams- nightmares, in fact. At first, he had ignored them... At least, he had tried to. But then it grasped him like a disease. Every single night, he would see the same dream, as if every night between 3 am and 3:30 am, he would delve into an untrue reality. It soon happened that he started feeling reluctant about attending weddings, that is, he started turning down the offers, afraid that his dream would become a reality someday. That girl- the bride in her dreams- her face became a reality to him, a reality in a dream he was not able to run away from. Soon came a time when he started believing that somewhere in the world, that girl actually existed. So, he would often stroll down the streets, scanning thoroughly the faces in crowd.

"I have to find her. She has all the answers to why all this is happening to me," he had told his therapist.

"It is just a dream, Dhruv. Do not let it alter your reality. We will find you a way out of it," Dr. Henna had softly

consoled him, *"But are you sure that you have not seen that bride girl in your life ever? You are a wedding photographer. Maybe she was one of your clients? Or try to remember, a classmate, a friend or some acquaintance? Anyone you ever came across... I would like to believe that she is someone you know or had known."*

"She isn't any client, I am sure. Once the dreams started, I too developed a similar doubt and so I took out all the wedding photographs I have clicked till date. A lot of work it was, but I... I just needed to be sure. And believe me, I neither found her as a bride or as a guest in any of the weddings I have attended. She cannot be anyone from school. In any case, the bride in my dreams is in her late twenties and I have not met anyone from my school after it was over, so she cannot be a schoolmate. I can assure you that she was no acquaintance before the dreams started... But now I feel that I know her... and that... I am connected to her somehow... and that she exists..."

"I understand what you say. I told you to meet an artist and describe the features of that bride girl. Did you do that?"

"I did it and he gave me the exact portrait of that girl. And as you told me to do, I showed that portrait to all my friends, relatives, neighbors, family and everyone. No one knows her. And none of them even remembers me mentioning any such girl."

"You see, Dhruv, there is an interesting theory in my field of work. It says that every individual is connected to a second individual on this planet. That is, even though these two individuals never have met or will never meet, they share a psychological connection. But it's a feeble theory with no proof as such, so let's stick to the proven science. I will give you some medicines, but I suggest that you take a break and go to

somewhere peaceful. You may go to the hills. Meditation is must for you, and one more thing- like always, keep a record of your dreams. And record your dreams fresh so that we don't miss upon on anything."

"Doctor, you may again take me under hypnosis."

"I would if it helped. Last time, it didn't reveal anything and I doubt if it will help now. Let us give it time because time reveals everything. Meanwhile, I will also do my research and try to find if any such chapel, as described by you, is known to exist."

And so, Dhruv was here, on the hills.

————◆◆◆————

Who says that a photographer's life is easy? A good photographer has to do a lot more than a normal human. A good photographer should be able to understand the emotions and expressions of the world so that her/his photographs can tell you the untold stories. A good photographer listens to the nature's voice; be it a bud blooming into a flower or the clouds cracking up to reveal the sun. And the photographer inside Dhruv had become restless since he came to the hills. Some days, he would wander far into the tribal villages to capture the ode of the human expressions, and there were days when he would roam around the hills, capturing the fabrics of the wonders of nature. It was his second week of stay and despite the fact that the nightmare still haunted him, he felt better here.

He was trying to capture a flock of colorful migratory birds over the lake and he kept moving towards their direction, lost in his photography. Many other tourists were also there and their number kept increasing. He was about to click a beautiful moment when he heard an irritated female voice calling out, *"Excuse me Mister, you are blocking my view."*

His hands shook and he could not capture what he was trying to. He too, in agitation, turned around as the female voice continued, *"Darn! I was trying to capture that moment for so so so long and now it is gone!"*

He turned back to see a camera fixed on a tripod angled to click the birds and then he saw a woman. She was looking down at her camera at the moment, perhaps checking if she had captured anything at all. Mumbling angrily, she looked up at Dhruv. He was heading towards her, apologizing in a meek voice. But his steps froze to an abrupt halt as his eyes caught the woman's face- the bride of his dreams, rather the bride of his nightmares; as flawless as she has been in his dreams. He stood there, horrified, as he looked at her. He felt weak in his head and something was going wrong in his stomach. He felt that he needed to sit down; no, he needed to lie down, he felt. But all he could do was just falling down. He needed to stand again, but his body didn't respond. He just waited there in panic; he waited for someone to pinch him and wake him up from the dream. The woman, perhaps, got scared as well by Dhruv's strange theatrical, and she, too, stood in silence for a while as she watched him fall down on his knees. She just waited, perhaps taking time to decide what she should do next. She, then, ran towards him to help him get back on his feet. She gave him some water and tried to calm him down.

"I just... it's just..." Dhruv could not decide what he should say. It was all just too awkward for him. He felt that a part of his brain was missing at that moment- the thinking

part. He looked around at the crowd of people who had gathered around him, *"It's nothing... just got a little dizzy... err... sleepless night..."* He tried to convince the crowd in an unconvincing tone.

"It's okay. Let's just go and see a doctor. It's just better... umm... you know if..." the woman fumbled but could not complete. She, perhaps, found herself in an awkward situation as well.

A couple minutes and a million of suggestions later, the crowd left Dhruv and the woman alone.

"Trisha," she stated, as she lifted up her camera and tripod, *"That is my name... aa... and you are?"*

Trisha gave Dhruv some support as they made their way to a local clinic.

"Dhruv." Dhruv finally felt the presence of some air to breathe. *"And... umm... don't mind, but are we somehow supposed to know each other?"* he asked, sounding slightly hesitating, *"I mean... No, this is not a sort of ice-breaker, I just asked because you look a little familiar."*

"Do I?" She looked at him, biting her lips. *"Well... I am not so sure... I don't think that we have met before."*

This followed an awkward silence for a while.

"So... Dhruv... What do you do, apart from these falling down stunts?" Trisha giggled with her attempts to soothe the growing discomfort.

"I am a photographer... a wedding photographer," Dhruv spoke.

"Are you?" she looked at him, startled.

"Yes, why? Why that disbelief on your face?"

She smiled as she looked around and then looked back at him. "*Oh! Nothing, it is just a rare thing to see a wedding photographer clicking the nature.*"

Dhruv uncomfortably chuckled as he replied, "*That is true. I have taken a break.*"

<hr>

The local clinic was in a precarious state. The doctor himself seemed to be in a dire need of treatment as he kept asking the same questions again and again, as if he was suffering from Amnesia. Dhruv and Trisha exchanged amused glances hearing the doctor's pathetically funny statements and recommendations.

"*Have you ever been to Mumbai? That is where I belong,*" Dhruv asked as soon as they came out of the clinic.

"*No... ummm... I was born and brought up in Vishakhapatnam. It's the first time I have ever come out of that place.*" Trisha smiled.

"*Oh! What do you do, by the way?*" Dhruv was still not over the shock of meeting his dream in reality.

"*Me? I do nothing actually... Photography is a hobby, so I am here,*" she spoke pointing at her camera.

"*Yeah, you should never stop clicking photographs; you never know how you will get your masterpiece.*"

"*Masterpiece?*"

"*Yes, that one photograph... the one you can call your success; the ultimate salvation of photography.*" Dhruv winked.

"*Success in one photograph? Impossible.*"

Dhruv sighed as he walked along with her, he felt like he was not with a stranger. He felt that he had known her for long and thus, the mist of discomfort was washing away now.

"My mentor, he was a famous photographer. He, like many others, used to decide on a topic and then he would wander for months, and he would visit places to click the right photograph for that topic. He, once, was trying to photograph 'Joy', and in search of the perfect photo, he kept wandering. One day, when he was developing photographs from negatives, he found his masterpiece that he had clicked- While trying to capture some lakeside view, the camera had captured his own reflection over the surface of water, and in that photo, he could see a smile round his lips- the joy of immersing oneself in what one loves to do. And that is the photograph he became famous for; the photograph that defined him- his masterpiece."

"Interesting story," she smiled and said, *"I am going towards the top; the crowd is less there and the chances that we get a masterpiece are high."* She winked.

"I was about to ask the same," he replied with a smile, *"but won't you be a little uncomfortable sharing your masterpiece with a stranger in that case?"*

"Hmmm... I never thought about that. But then, the best of life comes in the form of a stranger." A smile lit up her face. *"By the way... did you, by that statement of yours, mean to say that you wanted to get rid of me?"* she asked with a teasing expression.

"No... No... I didn't mean to..." Dhruv replied, growing cautious as Trisha chuckled and held his hand as they made their way towards the top.

Dhruv decided that he would keep silent about his dream for the time being. He did not want to freak her out. Moreover, he did not want to lose her. He saw her smile and it made him smile because in his dreams, he had only seen her cry. For a moment, he forgot about it all as he found the peace and comfort in her company that he had been looking for. As they made their way towards the top, the crowd kept mitigating and soon they could hear only the echo of each other's voice. She laughed and smiled and told him about her life. There was no way that she was related to him, it was clear to him by now. And yet, he felt that they were destined to meet. There were moments when he felt like holding her back in his arms, afraid that something terrible would happen to her.

They stopped at a place, exhausted, trying to catch some breath. They faced the valley and then, they faced each other. The cold wind echoed their silence. At this moment, Dhruv felt like he was looking at the infinity and the infinity was staring back at him. He was at peace. He was complete. All he saw was himself in Trisha's eyes. After a prolonged serene silence, Trisha's voice echoed.

"*May I tell you something?*" she asked him in a quivering voice.

"*Yes,*" Dhruv went cautious again.

"*This all may sound stupid to you and I don't intend to scare you either… but… I… I need to tell you. Promise me that you won't call me insane?*"

"*I will believe you… I promise.*" Dhruv was sure that nothing could be more unbelievable than the truth he was hiding.

"*You know… I…*" she paused, exhaled and continued, "*I am being haunted by this one nightmare for the past one year… In dreams, I see that I am sitting on the stairs of a chapel on my wedding day and in my arms… in my arms, I see my groom's*

corpse drenched in blood... I am never able to see his face...
it's so much soaked in blood. Then I..." She looked at Dhruv's
horrified face. "*Then I see you... with your camera... you
always want to tell me something... but she stops you...*"

"*She?*" Dhruv asked as he felt panic seeping into his
heart; his eyes went wide; they, now, had a glint of the
nightmare that he was expecting now.

"*Yes... a lady in black... dressed for funeral... and then
there is thunder and lightning and I wake up... you may choose
to disbelieve me... for words are my only proof... but I...*"

Dhruv stepped back. He could feel fear pumping into
his veins. He shut his eyes and pretended for a while that
he was still asleep, but his forced-nap was interrupted by an
apologetic cry.

"*I am extremely sorry for all this. But I can't help it,*"
Trisha continued, but Dhruv was not listening. His eyes
were fixed on her face; the face that had kept him awake
all this while; the face that he had known better than his
own; the face that he had been looking for in the mayhem
of strangers all this while.

"... We could possibly..." Trisha was still trying to
convince him.

He stopped her from speaking anymore and he placed
a finger on her lips as he wiped tears off her face. He too
wanted to tell her about his share of dream, but then... one
dream was enough for now.

She continued, "*It seems I have known you all my life...
I thought that I will lose my sanity and that you will be the
only reality I will be left with. I saw you down there and I
recognized you... you already seemed to be lost enough, so I
thought... I thought that I will slowly tell you about this...*

and I know that I am not taking it slow... but... I needed to tell you... I have known you all this while... I do not... I..."

"*I do not want to lose you,*" Dhruv completed as he took her in his arms.

They cried out the joy of finding each other. And then again, there was silence...

The silence was broken by the noise of a click. A camera clicked, and they opened their eyes to look in the direction of the noise. And their faces went white with horror.

A lady was standing with a camera. She smiled, waved at them and said, "*I am sorry for the intrusion, but this photograph might be my masterpiece.*"

She was not dressed like that, but both Dhruv and Trisha recognized her as the lady in black. They didn't realize when it had started drizzling. They looked above to see the black clouds hovering and they saw a chain of lightning strikes on the hill top. Beyond the mist on the slopes of the hill, they could now see a building in ruins; it looked like it was a church of some sort. The lady kept smiling at them. They were not sure if they had found each other in reality or right now, they were a part of someone else's dream. The storm kept building and the lady started walking away. Trisha and Dhruv drew each other closer, afraid that they would wake up again.

Miles apart, a woman woke up from a dream in an asylum. A smile dawned upon her ailing face as she mumbled, "*At last... They have found each other. There will be no more nightmares- nightmares that have haunted me for so long.*"

WRITER'S BLOCK

"*Writer's Block,*" Mukul mumbled in response when Mr. Pashupati asked him about how things were going.

"*You mean building, right? Writer's Building, the government building in Kolkata? Took a government job?*" Mr. Pashupati asked as he poured the gold-colored sanity into two glasses.

"*No,*" muttered Mukul, "*I mean Writer's Block only.*"

"*What's that?*" Mr. Pashupati asked with curiosity as he handed a glass of Scotch to Mukul.

"*I am not able to come up with a new story. No new ideas or new thoughts seem to enlighten me. It seems everything is stuck somewhere down there, but I am not able to reach them. It has been three months now. I think I am going through that phase known as a Writer's block,*" Mukul spoke as he emptied his glass.

"Bullshit! Come on, there is no such thing. How many bestsellers did you give in a row? Six?"

"Seven."

"And you are saying that you are not able to come up with ideas? It is all psychological. This writer's block or lock or whatever it is, there is no such thing." Mr. Pashupati tried to motivate Mukul.

"You are not a writer, so you won't know about it, Mr. Pashupati. And you won't know how frustrating and painful it is," Mukul blurted, *"You know, at times, I stay awake for days and nights, waiting to come up with some new thought, and just when I think I have a story, it is all gone... zooopp... blank again."*

"And, if I may ask, is that the reason you have started smoking again?" Mr. Pashupati pointed at the cigarette in Mukul's hand. *"As far as I remember, you completely quit smoking last year, right?"*

"Yes, I had to undergo a lot of medications, therapies, mental traumas and withdrawal syndrome to get rid of this," Mukul lifted up the cigarette as he spoke, *"but it, I believe, fuels the roots of my imagination."*

"It's such a pity when I see wise and learned men like you talking like this."

"It's not me; it's my frustration talking," Mukul promptly replied with a wink, *"See, what this Writer's Block does to people."*

"Again that block... I don't understand this; how can, all of a sudden, thoughts stop coming up," Mr. Pashupati mocked with a grin, *"It's all a myth created by writers as an excuse for not being able to come up with good work."*

"It is very easy for a banker to say that," Mukul spoke in an infuriated tone, *"Too easy... 'Not able to come up with good work' is exactly what happens during this phase, but it is not a 'myth'. Almost every writer, at some point of time, suffers from this. Many great writers have witnessed this pain."*

"Really?" Mr. Pashupati playfully looked at Mukul.

"Yes." Mukul lit up another cigarette as he extinguished the previous one. *"Have you heard of the book, 'The Great Gatsby'?"*

"Who hasn't?" Mr. Pashupati chuckled as he remarked, *"Especially after Mr. Amitabh Bachchan acted in that movie, everyone knows about it."*

"Yes," Mukul continued with a smile, *"the author of the book, Scott..."* he paused to remember the name and then said, *"Scott Fitzgerald went through a similar phase as well, and there are others like him."*

"The more you think that you cannot come up with any idea, the more will you feel the same. Thus, this affliction. You should give it some time. Just let it be for the moment. You will come up with something then." Mr. Pashupati placed the glass on the table with a loud bang, as if signifying his winning point in the argument.

"That is the point, Sir. We do not come up with ideas; ideas, thoughts, poems and stories... these all happen to us; we just ink them down." Mukul stood up, agitated. *"In a room of ten people, you see those ten people, but we see ten different stories. Thus, stories happen to us instantly, but nowadays..."* Mukul could not finish as his cellphone rang and he, in a hurry, picked received the call.

"Hello... Yeah... What? Come again... Died?" His face went grave and he immediately sat back on the sofa. *"How? He... but... he... I will go to his place immediately."*

"What happened?" Mr. Pashupati asked, sensing Mukul's grief.

"Koushik Biswas passed away," Mukul sadly mumbleded, still in disbelief.

"Koushik Biswas?" Mr. Pashupati took a moment to recollect, *"The writer Koushik Biswas? The one who wrote that brilliant book... what was it? Yeah, 'A cup of freedom' and 'In Absentia' and..."*

"Yes, the same one," Mukul murmured.

"Oh! That is such a big loss to India," Mr. Pashupati said with a deep sigh, not sure how exactly to react to the situation.

"The old man was my mentor," Mukul murmured in a very sad tone, *"You can say that he is the reason I am seen as a successful writer. When I last met him, he told me that he was working on his masterpiece. He was too excited about it. It was only last week that I visited him."*

"So, you want to go there now?" Mr. Pashupati queried, *"Would it be wise to go there... err... all drunk?"*

"Don't worry," Mukul answered as he lit yet another cigarette, *"I am in my senses. I need to go now."* Mukul stood up and scurried towards the door without even waiting for his host's approval.

It was an hour long drive to Koushik Da's house, and even though he kept telling the driver to speed up, it took him almost two hours because of the evening traffic. On his way, he kept thinking of the uncountable ways in which Koushik Da had helped him. From finding him his first publisher to editing his many flawed works, Koushik Da had done so much to help him. It was mostly because he treated Mukul like a son. His own sons were not interested in writing. His older son was a stock-broker and the younger one was pursuing some degree in science. It was not that Koushik Da was against their interests; he, simply, didn't have anyone to share literature with. And then, Mukul came to him with his zeal and talent.

His older son, Suraj, didn't like Mukul much and it was quite evident from the way he walked away when Mukul stepped into the house. Many famous faces were already in the house, mourning the author. Mukul also wiped off his tears as he heard the cause of death.

"Stroke," the younger son, Arka, told everyone as he fought to hold back his tears, *"For the past two years, he would quietly sit in his study without talking to anyone. If anybody asked, he would simply say, 'I am working on my masterpiece.' Today as well, he went and sat in his study. Our servant, Babu Da, went to give him his noon meal and saw him sleeping with his head over the desk. That was not an unusual thing, so he kept the meal on the desk and came back. Baba, as you already know, never liked to be disturbed again and again, so Babu Da usually used to collect the dishes during evening when he served tea to Baba. He did the same this evening. He found it odd to see Baba still sleeping. He shook him, but there was no response. It was then that he realized that something was wrong. We found him..."* Arka paused to hold back his tears, and then, he started again, *"He always used to say that he wanted to die amidst books and so he did."* He ran to another room, perhaps to avoid crying in front of everyone.

As was the tradition, Mukul touched the feet of his lifeless mentor who greeted him with an unresponsive, yet blessing demeanor. He was about to leave, but he thought it better to visit the temple before he left- Koushik Da's study. After all, his journey as a professional writer had begun from this study. So many old memories flooded in at once.

The term 'study' was a misnomer for this hall. It was more like a common room that was connected to all the other rooms. At the center of the room, sat a heavy old desk and a high-back, old-fashioned chair. On the desk rested a typewriter; most of the letters on the keys had faded away. On the desk, he noticed some bank papers and financial books along with the literature ones. This reminded him that Suraj, nowadays, used this desk for his office work as well and that the father-son duo would have occasional quarrels regarding the same.

He touched the typewriter, the chair and the desk and let his emotional deluge pay tribute to the great writer. He sat down on the chair and cried a little. Then, he stood up, realizing that it was getting late as he heard the voice of Koushik Da echoing inside his head, *"Do you know when a good time to cry is? Never."*

He was just about to leave when his eyes caught something- a black, leather-clad journal. *'Isn't it Koushik Da's journal? He said he was working on his masterpiece. Can it be the one? Yes, it's the same journal, I remember,'* he thought, *'But how does it matter.'* And he turned back to leave. *'But...'* his thoughts spoke up again as he looked back at the journal, *'No... No... No... What am I thinking? Stealing? That too from my Guru?'* He again looked away, sighed and started walking away. *'But he is no more. Who will take care of his unfinished work?'* he thought again as he took a few steps and slowed down his pace. *'Had he been alive, he definitely would have wanted me to take a look at it. And I am not copying his work, am I?'* He quickly turned back, walked up to the desk and slipped the journal into his bag. He looked around to see if anyone saw him. Even though his vision was blurred by Scotch and tears, he tried to look in all the directions. *'No one saw me,'* he whispered to himself, *'everyone is busy preparing for Koushik Da's last rites.'*

He quickly took leave from the house. After taking the journal, he was a bit afraid. After all, whatever may the excuse be, a thief always knows what wrong he has done.

He didn't stop anywhere else and straight away drove to his apartment. He didn't understand why, but when he got into the car, he felt that even the driver knew what he had done. As he got down from his car, the neighbors looked at him as if they also knew about it. He was not sure if everyone somehow knew about it, or if his guilty conscience made him feel that way. He checked his bag to see if the journal was visible somehow; or something, somehow, revealed what he had done. He couldn't find any. That is the problem after doing something wrong; you feel that everyone knows about it.

He locked himself inside his apartment and sighed with relief. By now, he was sober enough to think about it, so he took out the journal from his old worn out leather bag and looked at it. A strong feeling of remorse took a grasp of his body and he felt like killing himself right away. The scotch had also done its damage amidst all this. His head felt like being hammered from inside. *'I, bloody, need a bath,'* he murmured, clenching his teeth, restlessly walking around the table after keeping the journal on it.

The bath provided a little relief, but still, it didn't help him much. He realized that it was not a headache that was troubling him, it was guilt.

He quickly locked the journal inside an old cupboard, came out to the drawing room and switched on television. As he restlessly hopped from one channel to another, his mind kept hovering over the same thing again and again. It kept questioning him, *'Did you do the right thing?'*

'Why not?' he asked himself, *'I am not copying his work; I am only curious to know what his masterpiece is all about. I am not...'*

Frustrated, he switched off the television as his own thoughts vexed him, *'Why not? At most, I will just use the same idea as a base for my story. There is no wrong in it.'*

'It can't be a coincidence that I got my hands on this when I am suffering from this Writer's Block. It is a sign; a sign from God or a sign from Koushik Da himself. Maybe, they want me to complete his incomplete masterpiece. Maybe, if I once start, I will also get rid of this Writer's shitty Block' He stood up and briskly started pacing around the room. *'No, this is not a right thing to do. It is not my work. Even when no one knows, I will always know that it does not belong to me. I won't be able to savor the rewards. No, I can't do this. I have never even cheated anyone. How can I cheat my own self? All my ideas, my stories, no matter how they are, have been my own creations. They have, thus, been a part of me. A story written with the words of someone else can never be mine.'* He sat back on the couch and picked up the air-conditioner's remote to lower the temperature. He was sweating profusely.

'So what should I do? Should I simply go and return the journal to his sons? First, they will call me a thief and second, they won't understand the value of this piece of writing. It will lie there on the desk, talking to dust and cobwebs. It will never see light as a novel. I cannot let that happen. What should I do? Should I simply go ahead with writing a novel based on this? Yes, yes. That is a very good idea. I will get the novel published, and I will give proper credits to Koushik Da. Maybe, I will tell the world that the book is an outcome of long discussions between me and him, that he had a major contribution in my story... my story? That would be a lie. But this is a good idea. I will go ahead with it.' He stood up and walked into the room where the cupboard was kept.

Just as he inserted the key to open the cupboard, a thought came over and his momentarily lit up face went grim again. 'Won't the sons notice the missing journal of their father? What if someone has seen me?' He took out the key and walked back to his living room. 'Also, this Mr. Pashupati knows that I am suffering from Writer's Block. What will I tell him? I can't tell the world that all of a sudden, on the day Koushik Da's death, his ghost enlightened me with new ideas. They are all going to come back at me. I will lose my work, my dignity, everything.'

All of a sudden, a childhood memory struck him hard.

"I will become a thief, a burglar, when I grow up," he had told his father, expressing his frustration over regular studies.

His father had laughed and had replied, "That requires a stronger heart, a stronger determination and a stronger will. You won't be able to do it."

'How appropriate!' Mukul thought as he remembered his father's words, *'Thief... I won't be able to do it... But why not? Many great writers have used ghost writers, and many great writers and poets have copied works of others who either belonged to another country, or wrote in another language. Many of them are respected and worshipped as the best. Some are even known to produce better works than the original ones. If they can do it, why can't I?'*

He was now circling the entire room at a greater speed. *'The sons are least interested in their father's work. They, I don't think, will even bother to look for the journal. And if they do, the house was crowded with writers. No one has seen me taking the journal. I am sure I am as much a suspect as they are. Moreover, going by the affectionate relation between Koushik Da and me, I am going to be the least of all the suspects.'* This thought made him happy and sad at the same time, and he stood still by the window.

'Mr. Pashupati won't doubt me. Didn't he himself say that Writer's Block is just an excuse? He won't be surprised. In fact, he will be happy if I tell him tomorrow that a story has happened to me?'

'I shouldn't have gone today. This all wouldn't have happened then.'

Mukul decided to skip tonight's meal, though the maid had cooked his favorite fish preparation. At the moment, he felt as if his hunger, too, was blocked somewhere down there.

"If I am looking into the story and already stealing the concept, then won't it be better if I steal the whole story? Why should I do the rework? I need to come up with something while I am still not forgotten by my readers. I will definitely mention

in my book that Koushik Da helped me a little," he started speaking to himself again. *"In any case, I won't come up with a book all of a sudden; I will also recover from this 'Block' sooner if I already have a story. After all, it is all psychological, right? I will avoid all their suspicion by publishing this book a little late. Yes, I will."* His eyes gleamed with a dark light.

He walked up to the cupboard and opened it up. With shaking hands, he took out the book and brought it to his study desk, under light. With shivering hands, he held the book as he sat on a chair. Just when he thought that he would open the journal, his phone rang. He sprang up due to the sudden noise, getting his knee hurt by the edge of the table.

It was Mr. Pashupati.

"Mukul, how are you feeling now?" Mr. Pashupati spoke from the other side of the phone.

"I am okay," Mukul spoke in a rigid tone and coughed.

"You do not sound well. Are you sure you are alright? I mean... Take care of your health. I know that Koushik Biswas was a very close and fatherly person to you, but..." He paused for a moment, then he said, *"They are showing an old interview of his on this news channel. In the interview, he spoke about you as well. He praised you a lot. It seems he really loved you a lot. That is the reason I called you. If you..."*

Mukul did not let him finish. He hung up the phone. He tried to curse himself at a high pitch of voice, but he felt choked. The phone rang again, but he was not listening anymore.

'What was I thinking? This is not me. I can never steal from the person I respected the most. Just because he is dead, it doesn't mean that my respect for him also dies.' And with that,

he walked towards his desk. *'I will not only return this journal tomorrow, but I will also offer Koushik Da's sons help to get it published. If it is incomplete, I will help finish it… if and only if they allow me to do so. I will also follow the whole legal process required for the same.'* He smiled, finally.

'But till then,' he thought as he lifted up the journal, *'I am not going to read even a single word from this.'* And he slipped it back into his worn out leather back.

He peacefully slept like a child after that.

He woke up as he heard some vendor shouting on the street at the top of his voice. It was ten o'clock. He sat up on his bed and rubbed his eyes. Last night's incidents started playing in his head and he became sad as he smiled. *"Whatever has happened, I have just avoided a greater crime,"* he assured himself. He got out of the bed to start off with the morning.

He rehearsed his apology many a times in front of the mirror in his bathroom. He also rehearsed what and how he was going to speak about working on Koushik Da's work.

By the time he finished his late breakfast and got ready to leave, it was already mid-noon. He checked his bag once again to make sure that the journal was inside. He took the car keys and walked towards the door. Just as he was about to open the door, he heard the doorbell ringing. He opened the door, and with that, his face went white. It was Suraj, Koushik Da's elder son.

"Going somewhere, Mukul Da?" Suraj asked in a tone that froze Mukul's spine for a while.

"I… I… Actually, I was coming to your house…" Mukul fumbled a lot before he could complete. He motioned Suraj to come inside and said, *"I needed to talk…"*

"*I know why you were going to my house,*" Suraj interrupted, "*Is it in your bag?*"

"*Y... Yes... Yes...*" Shame and guilt took over Mukul's face as he took out the journal. "*I was coming to return it back.*"

"*That you had to, right? What would you do with my stock calculations?*" Suraj spoke in a mocking tone. "*Babu Da saw you keeping the journal in your bag last evening. He didn't say anything then because he thought it won't look good. Moreover, for the love of Baba, he did not want you to look like a thief... at least, at that moment.*" He took out another journal from his bag as he almost snatched away the one in Mukul's hands. "*You were probably looking for this journal- Baba's journal. Had you taken this, I wouldn't have bothered to drive this far. But you didn't look under the table. Baba's journal had fallen and it remained under the table.*" Suraj handed the journal to him as Mukul silently complied with disbelief, shame and guilt.

"*And... One more thing,*" Suraj spoke as he got up to go, "*I have received over a dozen phone calls since last night, all offering me a good sum of money in exchange for Baba's new book's manuscript, but still, I gave it to you. Do you know why?*"

Mukul didn't ask, but looked up.

"*I gave it to you because there is almost nothing in that journal. Except for a few pages in which he scribbled gibberish and himself chucked them off, mostly, there are blank pages. He used to say that he was not able to come up with new thoughts, ideas and stories. He kept blabbering about creating his masterpiece because he thought that it gave him hope. But in truth, he has not written anything in the past two years. What do you people call it?*" Suraj paused, trying to recall and said, *"Ah! Yes, Writer's Block; he used to say that he was suffering from Writer's Block. All silly excuses..."* He snorted as he walked out of the door, and on the couch sat Mukul, dumbfounded with his mouth agape.

HIS LAST STORY

The room, where they were sitting, had never been so quiet, and this made the guests feel uneasy. They were looking at him with concern, but Mr. McCarthy seemed to be too lost to notice them. His eyes were fixed at the window and the darkness beyond.

"*Mr. McCarthy,*" Mrs. Smith broke the silence, "*Are you alright?*"

Mr. McCarthy took a moment to answer, "*Yeah. Nothing, nothing... just this one something...*" his voice did the least to suppress his worry and fear.

Mr. McCarthy was the most respected person in this countryside town, not just because of his age, but also because of the acumen and knowledge he had acquired in his life full of quests and adventures, travelling round the globe. Everyone came to him seeking counsel on various matters and he helped them all, whatever the issue be. People often wondered how he knew so much because whatever might be the topic of conversation, Mr. McCarthy easily came up with his opinion backed up with facts and data. But that was kind of obvious.

At a very young age of twenty-three, he had left the comforts of home to explore the world. Even as an adolescent, he had known that a clerical job in an office was not what he wanted; he had always thirsted to explore the plethora of wonders that the world had to offer. His father, a merchant, had also bolstered Mr. McCarthy's wish with an abundance of wealth. And thus, soon, he was on his extraordinary pilgrimage of life. In this journey, he took up various jobs and various roles while visiting various places. From a job in diamond mines in Gauteng, South Africa, to setting sails with merchants over the Pacific to learning Ayurveda from the hermits in the Himalayas, he had done it all. But his lifelong adventure ended four years back when life greeted him with his new ride- a wheelchair. It was then that he had to return to his homeland, this town, and since then, he had been living in this old farmhouse his parents had left for him. Mr. McCarthy never married because he did not want to tie himself down. Now, he lived alone with a butler to take care of all his needs. His farmhouse was surrounded by corn fields, and during daytime, two workers used to come to take care of the fields. That was it; Mr. McCarthy had no other employees.

Of all the things that Mr. McCarthy was famous for, the most famous were his stories. And it was not that his stories were limited to a particular age group. It seemed that he had hundreds of thousands of stories for every age- may it be a child or an old man like himself. From the deep forests of Africa to civilization in Egypt to the birth of Politics in Rome to spiritualism of India to the mystery of El-Dorado to the literature submerged in the waters of Venice, he had stories about them all. And people would often visit him only to listen to his stories. In fact, Mr. McCarthy would often call people over his place to celebrate life; for that was the only adventure he sensed now. But the past two weeks had been a little strange for the town people. Mr. McCarthy seemed to have secluded himself from the others; at least, that is what people felt. Neither he gave, nor did he receive phone-calls. He didn't even allow anyone to visit him. If anyone came to visit him, Mr. McCarthy's butler, David, would turn him away saying that Mr. McCarthy was busy.

However, Mr. McCarthy had started a tradition of a monthly get-together with a few top-notch names of the town at his farm-house. These names were- Dr. Jones, The Wilsons, The Taylors, The Smiths and The Browns. Whatever the reason for his sudden seclusion was, he definitely did not seem to have forgotten this tradition as he had again sent invitations for dinner. The guests were also looking forward to see him because they were all concerned for Mr. McCarthy, and they wanted to know what had happened to him all of a sudden.

But since the moment they had arrived, the guests saw Mr. McCarthy silently staring out of the window. Never had any of them heard so much silence in this place. After all, this was the place where stories came into life.

Mrs. Smith decided to interrupt his thoughts and asked him if everything was alright, and Mr. McCarthy replied, *"Yeah. Nothing, nothing... just this one something..."*

"*What do you mean?*" Dr. Jones asked as he lit up his pipe, "*Is there anything I can help you with? I know that you yourself know a lot about medical science, but if any disease or something is troubling you...*"

"*No,*" Mr. McCarthy interrupted, "*No, no disease troubles me.*"

"*Then?*" Mr. and Mrs. Brown asked in an almost synchronized chorus.

Mr. McCarthy cleared his throat and muttered, "*I don't know if I should tell this to anyone but if you really want to know...*"

"*Blurt it out. That way we will be able to help. Or at least, you may feel a little relieved,*" Mr. Taylor said.

Mr. McCarthy started hesitatingly, "*Before I tell you this, I want to ask you all something,*" he dramatically paused, "*Do you think that something is wrong with me? Do you think that I have gone insane?*"

All exchanged startled stares and spoke in a chorus, "*No.*"

"*Hmm... See, I am telling you this and you have all the rights to mock me... mock... because I don't know if there is any way I can convince you. So, you can choose to believe whatever you want to.*"

"*What is it, Mr. McCarthy? Please speak. We believe you.*" Mrs. Brown spoke as she waited for others to affirm and then continued, "*We really want to help you.*"

"Alright," Mr. McCarthy lit a cigar as he started, "*It all started a few months back. One of the workers in my Corn Fields came to me and told me that he had found an abandoned scarecrow by the riverside. He told me that he had brought it to my farm and he asked for my permission to put it up in the fields. We didn't have any scarecrow in the farm and crows are* a real pest, so I gave him the permission. David showed me the scarecrow. It was exactly how a normal scarecrow is supposed to be. It was made of rugs and was stuffed with straw. I noticed that the rugs were torn, and the scarecrow itself looked so untidy and unwelcoming. I didn't want anything so unwelcoming in my farm. So I told David to repair it. And that is what David did. He replaced the untidy rugs with neat ones and made a new face for it. This new face had a warm, friendly smile on it. When David was done, it looked entirely different. In short, the scarecrow didn't scare me now. We had put it up at the middle of the fields, supported by bamboo, firmly fixed in the ground to withstand even storms.

Time started passing and I almost forgot about it. I forgot about it till one day. One day, my second worker came to me and asked, "Why is the scarecrow changing its place?"

I was expecting a visit from Dr. Jones that morning, so I did not entertain him much and sent him back to work.

Next day, both the workers came to me with worried faces. They said, "The scarecrow won't stand at one place. It is destroying the crops."

David chided them away. Both of us thought that the workers were making excuses for the poor yield of corn.

Now, all of you know that David takes me out on wheelchair every evening to get me some fresh air, right?"

Everyone nodded their heads in affirmation.

Mr. McCarthy coughed out smoke and then started again, "So, one evening, when I was coming back from my evening wheelchair-stroll, I got startled by what I saw. I told you that we had put up the scarecrow at the middle of the field where I used to see it every day, but at that moment, it was not there. I would usually ignore such things, thinking that one of *my workers is doing it for their convenience; after all, this is their farm as well. But then, I remembered what the workers had told me. I looked around and saw that the scarecrow was on the other side of the field. I asked David if he had done it, but he himself was appalled by what he saw. He told me that he didn't remember putting a scarf over the scarecrow, the one that we were seeing right then, around its neck. However, we did not let it play with our minds for long and got busy. Next morning, though, I called that worker who had brought it. He too sounded baffled and told that he knew nothing about the scarf or its movements. So, I started keeping an eye on the scarecrow. There would be days when it remained in its place, and there would be days when it changed its place. I was becoming obsessed with its movements. One day, I remember, while going out for my evening stroll, I noticed that it was in its place- in the middle of the field. It was not entirely dark by the time we returned, and I noticed that it was again missing. It had vanished. Out of habit and curiosity, I started looking around, but I could not see it anywhere. Just then, I felt like someone was watching me. I turned my head to look back. Just behind David, who was holding my wheelchair, there it was, dancing with the winds. Surprisingly, it was not there when we entered the farm. And I noticed one more thing, as did David, that its warm and friendly smile was gone. Now, the piece of rug was marred with a scarred smile and a pair of mischievous impish eyes. The whole sight gave us so much fright that we decided to take it down. Next morning, I told David to get rid of it and burn it down. I have travelled the world, but never have I come across such a thing. David got rid of it and he also burned it down... as he told me. But..."* he paused for a moment and again started as he looked out of the window,

"A couple of weeks back, when I woke up, David informed me that it was back again. He took me out and I saw it. Facing us, it stood in the middle of the field, and even from this distance, I could sense its scarred smile.

Not only that, one more thing has started in the past few days. I have been observing... and I feel... and I feel that... it is moving towards my house. In fact, in the past few days, it has moved closer and closer, and it is coming even closer..." Mr. McCarthy lifted up his hand and pointed towards the window. All the eyes in the room turned towards the window. Outside the window, a couple of yards away, in the dark, stood a scarecrow, apparently facing them.

Silently, they sat, exchanging petrified glances and they all turned towards Mr. McCarthy who was still looking towards the window.

"Actually, I believe you," Dr. Jones started, *"I have always seen the scarecrow in the middle of the fields. I noticed tonight that it was in a different place, but I thought..."*

"Yes, right," Mr. Smith spoke, *"Even I remember seeing it there."*

And everyone started looking towards the scarecrow again. Long moments of silence followed.

Silence was broken by a loud laughter which scared almost everyone. Mrs. Taylor dropped her glass of wine as she sprang up at the sudden noise. Everyone turned their heads to look at the source of this laughter- Mr. McCarthy. He just kept laughing as if he was overly amused.

"I am sorry... I am sorry..." Mr. McCarthy tried but could not stop laughing. David walked in and poured him a glass of wine which he finished in a single gulp.

He took a long drag of smoke to suppress his laughter and said, *"I am sorry about this all, but I just couldn't resist."*

"You mean... this was all..." Mrs. Smith started, a bit surprised, a little angry, somewhat amused and mostly relieved.

"A story?" Mr. McCarthy chuckled, *"Yes, indeed. You see, the scarecrow never moved anywhere. Today the workers were changing its location as they periodically do and it gave me this idea"* he laughed, *"After all, I had to come up with a nice idea for tonight's discussion, and what could be more interesting than making you all a part of the story? My apologies. I hope I didn't offend anyone of you, but look at your faces. Just look at your faces."* He continued laughing.

The guests exhaled in relief and they joined him in laughter.

"Then what about the scarf... or the change in its face?" Mrs. Taylor asked.

"Are you still thinking about it? The scarf was added today and the face never changed. It still bears that welcoming smile. If ravens understood smiles, they would never leave my farm, I swear," he winked as he continued, *"And no one found it abandoned anywhere. The workers themselves made it while I supervised."*

"Then what is reason of your worries for the past couple of weeks?" Mrs. Brown asked, smiling.

"Worry? Me? What are you saying?" It was Mr. McCarthy's turn to be surprised.

"Yes. You keep yourself secluded. So, we thought..." Dr. Jones started.

"So you all were thinking that it is related to this scarecrow?" Mr. McCarthy laughed again. *"Impeccable. Coincidences- that*

is why coincidences are so beautiful. But our lives themselves are nothing but aggregates of coincidences. The reason I had secluded myself is that I have decided to author a book. And I needed some solitude to contemplate on where should I begin with and that is why I kept to myself. But now that I have started and gained the momentum, I am back again."

Everyone congratulated him in a chorus and praised him.

Mr. McCarthy was overjoyed and he started speaking again, *"Whatever you may say, it was fun looking at all your scared faces. You really think that something as lifeless and as harmless as this..."* he stopped as his gaze turned towards the window and his eyes went wide with horror. He could not see what he was trying to point at- the scarecrow.

With a thunder, the door opened. All the eyes went towards the door, all eyes except for Mr. McCarthy's. He feared he knew what stood outside- a scarecrow with a scarred smile and hollow, evil eyes, dancing in the storm. Stories did come alive in this room.